Last Chance

A Last Healer Mystery
By Charles Huss

For my wife, Rose, who knows my faults and still wants to be with me.

Chapter 1

Jack Rosko approached the county jail and looked for a parking spot. The large gray building seemed to blend in perfectly with the gray sky. There were few empty spots, but he saw someone leave ahead of him, so he pulled his 2012 Ford F150 Crew Cab into the spot as a light rain dotted his windshield. The truck held memories of family road trips with his twin boys. Now that the boys were off to college, he didn't need such a big vehicle, but he liked having it. It made him feel powerful, almost as much as his police-issued Glock 19. His wife drove a small economy car, which, with his long legs, he found to be very uncomfortable. His parking spot was perfect. It was close enough to see who was coming and going from the jail, but far enough away not to draw attention to himself.

After a few minutes, Jack saw in the mirror one of those economy cars he disliked pulling into a spot two cars behind him. It was a gray Nissan Leaf. It was slightly bigger than his wife's car, but Jack couldn't understand the appeal of an electric car. He wanted to spend five minutes filling up at a gas station, not thirty. He wasn't against saving the environment, but giving up his luxuries was not going to make a damn bit of difference. What would help more would be if those movie stars stopped flying around in their personal jets while preaching about the environment.

He shook his head as he watched his partner, Bill West, get out of the car. He grew tired of pretending to like the guy. When he approached, Jack lowered his window.

"Hi, Jack," Bill said. "I thought I'd find you here. So, this is how you are spending your vacation? I would have thought you would enjoy a trip to the Dells more than sitting outside a jail."

"Hey, Bill. Are you here to arrest me, or are you my babysitter now?"

"No. I was just concerned about you," Bill said as he put both hands on Jack's door and leaned in a little. "Don't you think you're taking this a bit too personally? You should let it go. The guy did his time. It's not your job to harass him after he gets out."

"First, I'm not harassing him. Second, why do you care? Third, five months in jail is hardly a punishment for stealing two hundred thousand dollars' worth of jewels. I just want to set things right."

"We investigated the case and never found the jewels. What did you expect the prosecutor to do? The only charge he could bring against him was breaking and entering."

Jack's pulse quickened, and his grip on the steering wheel tightened as he raised his voice. "Do you think it's right that he spent five months in jail and walked away with two hundred grand? That's forty grand a month. That's way more than I make. It feels like he's rubbing it in our faces. We've both been doing this job for over twenty years. Don't you ever get tired of doing all the work to bring these assholes to justice only to have them back on the streets a few months later doing the same shit?"

"Of course, I do, but we're just little cogs in a big machine. The best we can do is accept the reality and try to be happy with what we have."

"I joined the police force to make a difference, but I'm not the same man I used to be. The system has beaten me down," Jack said.

"So, what do you plan to do?"

"I know he hid the jewels somewhere. He won't be able to resist and will lead me right to them."

"What will you do then?" Bill asked. "If you find the jewels, will you keep them? Will you turn them in so some rich politician can have them back?"

"I will do what needs to be done," Jack said.

"You asked me why I care. I'll ask you the same thing. Why do you care? You have a week off. You should be spending it with your wife. Instead, you're neglecting her."

"Don't assume you know my wife. She cares about justice just as much as I do."

"Justice for who? For him or for you? People get away with crimes every day in this city. What makes this guy so special?"

"Have a good day, Bill," Jack said before raising his window. He didn't want to talk anymore. He wanted to do something for a change that didn't require following procedure.

Bill stood outside Jack's window for several seconds before he returned to his car and drove away.

Ten minutes later, a blue, older model Chevy Impala rolled up in front of the jail and parked. The female driver kept the motor running and waited. Jack turned on his wipers so he could see better.

After what seemed like an hour but was really closer to five minutes, a thin, middle-aged man exited the jail holding a small plastic bag, probably what he had on him when he was arrested. Even from a distance, Jack recognized the man as Bobby Parker. He watched Bobby enter the car and lean over to kiss the driver.

When the car pulled away, Jack started the engine and followed. They drove for twenty minutes, finally reaching the home of Bobby and his wife. Jack parked a few houses down and watched as Bobby helped his wife out of the car. She looked very pregnant - more than eight months, Jack guessed.

The house was a modest one-story home painted white with dark red trim. It needed a fresh coat of paint, but it still seemed in decent shape. Jack watched as Bobby helped his wife up the steps and into the house.

He waited almost an hour until Bobby emerged from the house alone, got in the car, and drove away. Jack followed him but kept his distance. They headed northwest on the highway for about an hour and a half. Jack had guessed where Bobby was going, but knew for sure when he exited. He decided to back off just in case Bobby suspected someone was following him. He slowed until he could no longer see the Impala in front of him. He also didn't see the car that followed him.

***

Michael Owens, the Three Eagles Ski Resort manager, stood behind the counter when Bobby Parker walked inside. A friendly-looking middle-aged man with salt and pepper hair, Michael's warm smile always put a guest at ease. "Hello," Michael said. "Welcome to Three Eagles."

"Hi. My name is Robert Parker. My wife reserved a room for me."

Michael hit a few keys on his computer and said, "Oh, yes. I see you here. It looks like you are a returning guest. Welcome back, Mr. Parker."

Bobby coughed and said, "Thank you."

"The reservation is for one night. Is that correct?"

"That's right," Bobby said.

3

"Great. The ski season is over, but we still have plenty to offer. Mountain bikes are free to use, or you can rent an ATV. You may also enjoy spending time in the hot tub. Here is your key. It's for room 109, just down the hall and to the left. Do you need help bringing in your luggage?"

"No, thanks. I have no luggage," Bobby said before he turned and walked to his room.

As Bobby left the front desk, Jack Rosko entered the lobby. At a little over six feet tall, with broad shoulders and thick, dark hair with a few white strands running through it, he exuded a rugged charm. He watched Bobby disappear down the hall before approaching the desk.

Michael smiled at him and said, "Welcome to Three Eagles. Do you have a reservation?

"No, I don't. Do you have a room available for tonight?"

Michael checked his computer and said, "I can give you room 207. It has a great view of the slopes. Even though the snow is gone, it looks lovely in the spring."

"Do you have a room on the first floor?"

Michael hit a few keys and said, "I'm sorry, I'm afraid all the first-floor rooms are booked for today."

"No Problem. I'll take what you have."

"Okay. I'll need a driver's license and a credit card."

Jack opened his wallet and handed over the cards. As Michael entered the information, he asked, "Have you stayed with us before, Mr. Rosko?"

"No. I was here once but didn't spend the night."

Michael told him about everything available to do at the resort and handed Jack his driver's license and credit card back before giving him the keys. "Your room is on the second floor. Take the elevator and turn left when you get off. Can I get someone to help you with your luggage?"

"No. I don't have any luggage," Jack said as he walked away.

That's odd, Michael thought as he watched him leave.

A minute later, another man entered. He looked to be in his late thirties. He was thin with short dark hair and a well-groomed beard. He walked up to Michael and said, "Hi. My name is Jay Lawrence. I don't have a reservation, but I hope you have a room available tonight."

"We do, but they're going fast today. I can give you room 210 on the second floor."

"That will be fine," The man said.

Michael checked him in and told him about the resort. He then asked if he needed help with his luggage.

"I don't have any luggage," Jay said.

What the hell is going on around here, Michael thought.

***

After entering his room, Bobby used the washroom and then washed his face. He checked himself in the mirror. These last six months had been rough on him, and it showed. His once-dark hair had started turning gray. His skin was dry and pale, with dark circles under his eyes. He sighed, sat on the bed, picked up the phone, and dialed a number. "I'm at the resort," he said when it was answered. "No. I haven't checked yet, but I will soon. Hopefully, it's still here. Okay. I'll be careful."

After hanging up, he decided it was time to get what he came for. He walked to the door, opened it, and was met with a gun pressed against his chest. "Oh, Shit!" Bobby said.

The man holding the gun pushed him back inside and closed the door. "You sound surprised, Bobby," he said.

"I figured he would send someone sooner or later. I was hoping for later."

"Nobody ever got what they wanted by hoping. Now, tell me where the jewels are?"

"Jewels? What jewels?"

"Don't give me that crap. You know what jewels I'm talking about.

"I have no jewels," Bobby said.

"This is the only place you could have hidden them. Where are they?"

Bobby studied the man's face and said, "You really don't know, do you?"

"Know what? What are you talking about?"

"You dumb son of a bitch," Bobby said and laughed.

The man pressed his gun hard into Bobby's chest and said, "I'm glad you can find humor in your situation. You know he wants you dead, right? He sent me here to kill you. I can tell him that you gave me the slip. Just give me the jewels."

"You realize the man you work for is a paper tiger, right? He could have had me killed in jail, but he doesn't have the power or influence to do something like that."

"Maybe he just figured waiting until you got out would draw less attention to your death."

"Maybe he's not as smart as he thinks he is."

"This is your last chance."

Bobby looked at the man with disdain. "He will fall, and you will fall with him."

"Maybe so, but you will fall first," the man said before pulling the trigger.

Bobby fell to the ground. The man checked his pockets but found nothing. He then quickly searched the room, opening every drawer and cabinet.

Eric, Michael's son, was in the hallway when he heard the shot. At first, he thought it was someone playing the television too loudly, but after listening for several seconds and hearing nothing further, he worried someone had committed suicide or at least attempted to commit suicide. He knocked on the door but got no response. He knocked again, but still no response. He took out his master key and opened the door. He cautiously looked inside. The room was relatively dark, lit only by the light coming through the window at the far side of the room. Even so, he could see a man lying on the floor in a pool of blood.

His heart quickened as he raced to the man, knelt beside him, and checked for a pulse. The man opened his eyes, grabbed Eric's arm, coughed once, and said, "Number three."

"Number three? What does that mean?"

Before the man could respond, everything went dark.

***

The phone rang at the front desk, and Michael answered it. He saw it was an internal call. "Front desk. How can I help you?"

"Hi. I'm in room 111," a female voice said. "I just heard a gunshot in the room next to me."

"A gunshot?" Michael said, shocked. There had never been a shooting at Three Eagles since he had been there. "Are you sure that's what you heard?"

"I'm not positive, but that's what it sounded like."

"Okay. Thanks for letting us know," he said before hanging up. He walked quickly to see what had happened. He stopped before turning the corner, just in case there was someone there with a gun. Seeing no one, he continued down the hall until he came upon room 109. The door was open. He cautiously looked inside and saw Eric lying on the ground next to a man covered in blood. His heart skipped a beat.

"Eric! Oh, my God!" he said, racing to his side. He pressed the side of his neck, looking for a pulse. Just then, Eric opened his eyes.

"You're alive! Oh, thank God!" Michael said before hugging him.

Eric sat up and rubbed his head, "Dad? Where am I? What happened?"

"I was going to ask you that."

Eric turned and saw the body. "Oh, my God! Is he dead?"

Michael checked for a pulse and said, "I'm afraid so."

"I remember now. I heard a gunshot," Eric said. "I opened the door to see what happened and found him lying there. When I checked on him, he said something about 'number three,' and then someone hit me from behind."

"Number three? What does that mean?" Michael asked.

"I have no idea. I asked, but someone knocked me out before he could reply."

Michael took out his phone and asked, "Are you okay? Should I call an ambulance?"

"No. I'd rather have grandpa look at me."

Michael nodded and dialed 911. He reported the murder and then dialed Katie's number. She and Joe were helping Katie's friend in Milwaukee, but Michael knew they would be wrapping things up and returning home soon. Katie answered and said, "Hi, Michael."

"Hi, Katie. Is Pops with you?"

"He's right here. Just a minute. You're on speaker."

"Hi, Pops. I'm sorry to interrupt what you are doing there, but we have a problem at the resort."

"What kind of problem? What happened?" Joe asked.

"Someone was murdered."

"Murdered?" Katie blurted out. "Tell me you're kidding."

"I'm afraid not. A guest I just checked in was shot in his room. Eric was hurt, too. The killer, I assume, hit him on the head."

"Oh, No!" Joe said. "Is he okay?"

"I'm okay," Eric said. "I just have a big headache."

"We're leaving now," Joe said. "Hang tight, Eric. You'll be feeling better in no time."

***

When the killer was far enough away, he took out his phone and dialed a number. It was picked up on the third ring. "Did you take care of our little problem?"

"Yes. He won't be an issue anymore."

"Did you find what he went there for?"

"He didn't have the jewels. I searched his room."

"Jewels? The jewels don't concern me. I told you to find what he went there for."

"What else would he have hidden here if not the jewels?"

"The man on the other end of the line told him what he should look for."

"I wish you had made that clearer to me before. I'll hang around here to see what I can learn, but it's doubtful he can hurt us from six feet under."

"Do you want to take that chance?"

"I suppose not, but what about the jewels?"

"If you find any jewels, feel free to keep them," the man said before hanging up.

"Shit!" he said to himself. "I don't get paid enough for this crap."

Chapter 2

Katie and Joe felt good after solving a string of murders and saving several lives, including Katie's friend Ashley and two terminally ill patients, despite having a close brush with death less than a day earlier. Just before Michael's phone call, they decided to forget about solving murders and commit themselves to healing people, but murders seemed to have a way of finding them.

They left the hospital, where they had saved a woman in need of a new heart, and quickly got on the road.

"I hope Eric will be okay," Katie said. "I mean, I know you will make sure he is okay physically, but getting attacked by a murderer has got to have a mental effect on someone."

Joe reached over and held Katie's hand, reassuring her with his touch. "We haven't talked much about what happened yesterday. Are you okay?"

Tears welled up in Katie's eyes. She wiped them away. "I don't know. I can't stop thinking about what almost happened. At the time, I didn't think about myself at all. All I could think was I couldn't die knowing the baby would die with me."

"That's understandable. You put the welfare of the baby above your own welfare. You thought exactly the way a great mother would think. You were worried about what kind of mother you would be the other day, and I think this proves you will be wonderful."

Katie shook her head. "No. I'm a terrible mother. I put myself, you, and the baby in danger. We should have gone home when Ashley was better."

"I think we both played a part in that decision," Joe said. "If we didn't stay and finish the investigation, Robertson would still be out there killing innocent people. Also, if we had gone home earlier, you might have been hit on the head instead of Eric, and I don't think you have a hard head like he does."

Katie laughed.

"That's what I like to see," Joe said.

"I'm afraid a joke won't make me feel better."

"I know, Honey. Only time will do that."

"Don't call me 'Honey.' That's what Robertson called me before he tried to kill me."

"I'm sorry. How about 'Darling' or 'Sweety' or 'My Love' or maybe 'Pumpkin?'"

"Those will work, except 'Pumpkin.' Never call me 'Pumpkin.'"

"Okay, Darling. Just know I'll always be here for you. I'll listen whenever you feel sad or anxious and want to talk."

Katie squeezed Joe's hand and said, "I know you will. That's why I love you."

She looked at Joe momentarily and asked, "What about you? You killed a man. That must be hard on you. I remember when I almost killed you. Even not knowing you at the time, I would have been devastated if I were responsible for killing you."

"I did it to save you, and I would do it again if I had to. I wish it weren't necessary to kill him, but I don't regret it. Robertson was a murderer."

"So, you're okay?"

"I'm okay, but I am a little concerned."

"Concerned? What are you concerned about?"

"I touched a man and stopped his heart. It's a power I'm not sure I want to have. I was starting to enjoy having the ability to save people's lives, and now I learn I can also cause their deaths. What if I misuse this ability? What if I kill someone out of anger?"

Katie shook her head. "No. Not you. I haven't seen you angry since I met you. Having your ability is like carrying a loaded gun. There are plenty of people who carry a gun everywhere they go without ever drawing it on anybody, and you are probably more even-tempered than most of those people."

"I hope you're right."

"Don't worry. I know you're a good man. Two people called you an angel when we were in Milwaukee, and I'm starting to believe it might be true."

"Really? You mean an actual angel from heaven?"

"Is that so impossible? How do you explain your abilities? What if one of your ancestors mated with an angel? That would make you part angel, anyway." Katie had kept those thoughts to herself, but now they were out in the open. She worried Joe might think she was crazy.

"You don't seriously believe I'm part angel, do you?"

"I don't know if I believe it or not. I just haven't ruled it out."

"Part of me wants to laugh at your suggestion, but you're right. I can't explain my abilities. I don't know if they evolved naturally or were somehow given to me by a higher power. If I am part angel, I might have some explaining to do when my time is up."

Katie laughed. "You're joking, right? Your biggest sin is leaving the toilet seat up."

"That's not true. I once tore a label off a mattress."

Katie laughed and held Joe's hand tight. "The origin of your abilities may be one mystery we will never solve, but it doesn't matter to me where you came from. I'm just glad you're here now."

"I feel the same way about you."

Do you think we will ever have that normal life we talked about?"

"Well, you were concerned that normal would be boring," Joe said. "If things keep going the way they're going, you'll never be bored."

"That's an understatement."

***

The drive to the resort took about two hours, but it felt longer this time. It felt almost as long as the drive to Milwaukee a week earlier, when Katie's friend, Ashley, was near death after being shot.

Despite its age, the resort was well-maintained with an old-world charm. The large wooden structure at the bottom of one of Wisconsin's tallest peaks looked majestic, like a palace where a fairy-tale princess would live. Several sheriff's deputy cars blocked the front entrance, so Katie found a spot in the parking lot.

A pleasant scent of pine and cedar drifted on a light breeze as they walked toward the entrance. The lobby was inviting. It also had an old-world charm with plenty of antique furniture that encouraged guests to hang out and converse or read a book while sipping coffee.

They found Michael and Eric chatting behind the front desk. Sitting near a window and conversing separately were Michael's wife, Sarah, and Eric's wife, Rachael. In her mid-forties, Sarah was fit and trim, with long legs and silky dark hair. In her early twenties, Rachael was young and pretty, with medium-length blonde hair. She held her baby daughter while they talked.

Katie's eyes lit up when she saw the baby, who smiled and moved her arms back and forth when Katie approached. "Hello, everyone," she said before returning her attention to the baby. "Oh my, she looks bigger every time I see her. How old is she now?"

"Eleven weeks," Rachel said, smiling.

Katie held out her finger, and the baby grabbed it. Katie smiled. "Oh wow! You have quite a grip there, little Molly. I bet you'll be an athlete when you grow up."

She turned to Joe, excitement in her eyes. "Isn't she adorable? I can't wait to have one of our own."

"Speaking of that," Joe said, "would you like to tell everyone, or should I?"

"Tell us what?" Sarah asked, her curiosity piqued.

"This is probably a bad time to bring it up, but we're going to have a baby," Katie said.

Sarah's face lit up. "That's fantastic," she said as she stood up. "Congratulations." She hugged both of them tightly. "This is not a bad time to tell us. We need some good news."

Everyone congratulated Katie and Joe. When the fuss died down, Eric said, "I saw your story this morning, Katie. It was impressive how you two solved those murders. I bet it was a bit scary, too."

Katie nodded, "Thanks, Eric. Yes, there was a terrifying moment at the end, but we survived, thanks to Joe."

Joe looked puzzled. "How did you see Katie on television? We don't get Milwaukee stations up here."

Eric laughed. "I didn't see her on television, Grandpa. I watched her on my phone."

"That thing gets television stations?"

Katie put her arm around Joe and said, "I'll explain it to you later, Mr. Van Winkle. Right now, don't you have some healing to do?"

Joe's expression turned serious, remembering what he needed to do. "Oh, yes. Of course." Joe looked at Eric and asked, "How are you feeling, Eric?"

Eric rubbed the back of his head and said, "I feel a little better, but it still hurts, and I feel lightheaded sometimes."

"You might have a concussion. Let's go into the office and see if we can fix it," Joe said, leading the way.

Eric sat on Michael's chair as Joe pulled the chair from his desk and sat beside him. He held Eric's hand and thought of him as an extension of his body.

Soon, he could feel what was wrong inside Eric's body. Eric could feel it, too. They were connected as one person. They couldn't read each other's thoughts but could feel what was happening inside their bodies.

The feeling of being connected to another person while feeling everything from the inside was impossible to describe. Only through experiencing the Healer's touch could one truly understand. Joe and Eric could both feel the damage that occurred to Eric's brain near the injury. There was a small amount of bruising and swelling.

After learning how to heal others, Joe used his gift to bring all his family members to optimal health, so Eric knew what to expect. Joe spent about ten minutes healing Eric. When satisfied, he let go and said, "It's not a hundred percent, but you'll be fine. I can do more later if you need it. Let's join the others and talk about what happened."

They returned to the lobby, where two deputies stood by the front desk next to a woman in plain clothes. She was about forty, with straight, dark hair tied behind her head. She wore black slacks and a white blouse. Her badge hung from her waist. Michael introduced her, "Joe, this is Detective Connor. Detective, this is my other son, Joe Novak."

"Oh, you have a different last name."

"I was adopted," Joe said. "I kept my real parents' last name."

That was mostly true. Joe was adopted, and Novak was the last name of his birth parents, but his real adoptive parents both died before Michael was born.

Detective Connor looked surprised. "Really? You and Eric look so similar. You are both tall with the same dark brown hair and brown eyes. I would swear you two were related."

"It is quite a coincidence," Joe said.

The detective reached out her hand and said. "Well, it's nice to meet you, Mr. Novak."

They shook hands, and Joe smiled. "Call me Joe. 'Mister' makes me feel old."

Katie found that funny and tried to hold back a laugh as the detective said, "You have a long way to go. I have kids almost as old as you."

The urge to laugh was too great, so Katie turned her head to hide her face.

Joe saw what she was doing, reached over, and quickly tickled her side. Katie couldn't hold it and let out a big laugh.

Detective Connor looked confused and asked, "Did I say something funny?"

"No. It's my husband. He can be quite annoying sometimes," Katie said.

"Oh, yes. I have one of those, too. Now, I have a few questions for Eric."

"Okay. I assume you want me to tell you what I saw," Eric said.

"Yes. Start from the beginning, and don't leave anything out, no matter how trivial you think it might be."

"Okay. I was in the hallway near room 109 when I heard what sounded like a gunshot. My first thought was to ask the guest to turn his television down, but the room was quiet when I stopped to listen. I then worried that the guest might have shot himself. I've heard about people committing suicide at hotels, but I never experienced it here. I knocked on the door. I waited a few seconds for a reply and then unlocked it.

"When you unlocked the door, were you not concerned that someone else might be there?" Detective Conner asked.

"I should have been more worried," Eric said. "The thought crossed my mind, but I foolishly focused on it being a suicide attempt."

"So, what happened next?"

"I opened the door and saw the man lying on the floor with blood all around him. I didn't see anyone else in the room, so I rushed to his side. I checked for a pulse, but before I could feel one, he opened his eyes, grabbed my arm, and said, 'Number three.' I asked him what that meant, but someone hit me on the head. I remember nothing after that."

"Number three?" Joe said. "So, you don't know what he meant by that?"

"I have no idea."

"Could it be a room number?" The detective asked.

"All our room numbers are three digits," Michael said.

"Do you have any cameras here?" Connor asked.

"I'm afraid not," Michael said.

"I've been thinking about having cameras installed," Joe said. "I guess I procrastinated too long."

"I guess you did," Connor said.

"So, who was the victim?" Katie asked.

"His name was Robert Parker," Michael said. "He just checked in ten minutes before he was shot."

"We are looking into his record. We should know more soon," Connor said.

"Robert Parker," Katie said. "That name sounds familiar."

"Do you know who he is?" Joe asked.

Katie thought for a moment and said, "No. I don't know him personally, but we did a story about a guy with the same name around six months ago. Can I see the body?"

"Are you sure you want to? It could be disturbing," Detective Connor said.

"No, I'm not sure. Let's do it before I change my mind."

"Okay. Follow me."

Katie and Joe followed her to room 109. A couple of deputies were in the hallway talking to guests. One deputy dusted the doorknob for fingerprints as they walked into the room. Katie looked at the body lying on the floor. After a couple of seconds, she turned her head and said, "It's him."

"Let's talk outside," Joe said. He held Katie's hand as they walked into the hallway. Connor followed them and asked, "Who is he?"

"He was arrested for breaking into the home of Timothy Ford."

"Timothy Ford? I've heard that name somewhere before," Connor said.

"He's the mayor of Milwaukee," Katie said. "Senator Scott is retiring, and he's running to replace him."

"Oh, that's right. That's where I heard the name."

"Anyway, they say Parker stole about two hundred thousand dollars' worth of jewels, which they never recovered. They couldn't charge him with robbery because they couldn't prove that he stole anything, but the police recovered his fingerprints inside the house, so they charged him with breaking and entering."

"That story sounds so familiar," Joe said. "What was the victim's name again?"

"Robert Parker," Detective Connor said.

"When did the robbery happen?"

Katie looked it up on her phone and said, "It happened on November 4th last year."

"Let's go talk to Michael," Joe said, leading them back to the front desk.

Everyone was still in the lobby, and now Susan had joined them. Susan was Michael's mother and Joe's daughter. She was around eighty but seemed quite a bit younger, except for her thick white hair. She hugged Joe and then Katie. I heard what happened, and I'm sorry to hear about your friend's mom, but I'm glad your friend is okay."

"Thanks so much, Susan," Katie said. "Joe is a miracle worker."

"He is special," Susan said. "I also heard about the baby. I'm so happy for you both."

"Thanks again. I may be asking you for parenting advice in the near future."

Susan smiled. "Don't forget you are married to a man who raised three children."

"He raised them as a dad. I need advice from a mom."

"Of course. I will be here for you, Dear."

Joe turned to Michael and said, "Do me a favor and see if Robert Parker was here on the fourth of November."

Michael typed a few keys, looked at the screen, and said, "Yes. He was here that day. How did you know?"

"Do you remember the police coming and arresting him?"

"No, I don't. That was a Saturday during the off-season. I was probably home that day."

"I remember," Eric said. "I didn't realize that was the same guy, but I remember several Milwaukee police officers taking him away."

"I remember that, too," Joe said. "I wonder why he would return here."

"Maybe he hid the jewels here," Katie suggested. "I remember the judge sentenced him to five months in jail. Maybe he got out recently and returned to retrieve the jewels from where he hid them."

"That makes a lot of sense," Connor said.

"What room did he have the last time he was here?" Joe asked Michael.

Michael tapped a few keys and said, "He was in room 203."

"Did he request that room again?" Joe asked.

"No. I took the call. Parker's wife made the reservation for him but made no special requests. He also said nothing about wanting a specific room when he arrived."

"I would think if he hid the jewels in his room, he would ask for the same room," Katie said.

"Is that room available now?" Detective Connor asked.

"Yes, it is," Michael said. "Would you like to see it?"

"Yes, I would," she said.

Michael picked up a master key and handed it to Joe. "Can you show it to her? I need to stay here."

"Certainly," Joe said. "Follow me."

Detective Connor, Katie, and a deputy followed Joe to the second floor. He unlocked the door, and they all went inside. The room had a single king-size bed positioned against the left wall, with a nightstand on each side. A small table and a couple of chairs stood beside the bed on the side nearer to the door. There was also a writing desk against the right wall. A sliding glass door led to a small balcony at the room's far end.

Everyone looked around the room for places where someone could have hidden jewels. Katie began to pull out the nightstand drawers. She turned each of them upside down to ensure nothing was taped to the bottom.

Joe looked on the balcony for any potential hiding places. He took the cover off the light fixture and felt inside for anything that shouldn't be there. An eight-foot gap separated each balcony, so hiding the jewels on the next balcony was virtually impossible.

The young deputy checked under the mattress while the detective searched the closet. "This is pointless," she said. "I'm sure this room was checked from top to bottom when Parker was arrested. Besides, he probably already retrieved the jewels, and the person who shot him has them now."

"I don't think so," Joe said. "I noticed every closet and every drawer was open in that room. The killer was looking for something, and unless he got lucky and found what he was looking for in the very last possible place, he left empty-handed."

"What if he searched the room first and then tortured the information out of Parker before shooting him?" Katie asked.

Joe looked at Detective Connor and asked, "Did you see any signs of torture?"

"I didn't notice any bruising or anything like that. The coroner's office will pick up the body any minute now. After the medical examiner does the autopsy, he can tell us for certain."

They left the room, and Joe closed the door behind them. They continued their conversation as they headed back to the front desk. A man approached them, showed a badge to the detective, and said, "Hi. I'm Sergeant Jack Rosko of the Milwaukee Police Department. Are you in charge here?"

"Yes. I'm Detective Connor. What can I do for you?"

"The man who was killed here, Robert Parker, is a suspected jewel thief. We believe he hid the jewels here and returned to retrieve them after he was released from jail. I was sent to find the jewels and return them to the rightful owner."

"Who happens to be the mayor of Milwaukee," Katie said.

"That's right. How did you know that?"

"I spent time in Milwaukee as a news reporter," Katie said.

He looked at her and said, "I thought you looked familiar. You did those human interest stories. Channel 12, right?"

"Channel 23," Katie said. "I got promoted to investigative reporter."

"Oh, yeah. That's right. Channel 23. Sorry, but I don't watch the news much. Are you here on vacation?"

"No. I live here now."

"I envy you. It's a beautiful place."

"Tell me," Joe said, "how is it that the mayor of Milwaukee has such an expensive collection of jewels in his home?"

"Timothy Ford's father was very successful in the jewelry business. He retired about ten years ago, and Timothy took over the company. That was a few years before he became mayor," Jack said. "He has one of the Midwest's most successful jewelry store chains. I'm sure you've heard of Ford Jewelers."

"No, I haven't," Joe said.

"I have," Katie said.

"So, what exactly do you want from me, Sergeant Rosko?" Detective Connor asked.

"Have you found any signs of the missing jewels during your investigation?"

"No, we haven't."

"Did you search the room where the body was found?"

"It looks like the killer searched the room before we arrived, but we plan on doing a thorough investigation."

"I would like to help you search the room," he said.

Detective Connor considered his request for a moment and said, "No. This is not your jurisdiction. My team is competent. If we find anything, we will let your captain know. Do you have a business card?"

Jack Rosko hesitated but opened his wallet and took out a business card. He handed it to Detective Connor, who looked at it and said, "We'll be in touch."

He started to say something but stopped, put his wallet back in his pocket, said, "Thank you for your time," and walked away.

"I can't put my finger on it, but there is something off about that guy," Connor said.

"I thought so, too," Katie said.

They returned to the front desk, where only Michael remained.

"Where is everyone?" Joe asked.

"With everything that has happened, nobody has had a chance to eat lunch, so they went to the restaurant."

"They left you behind?"

"I told them to go. Someone has to watch the front desk. Did you see that Jack Rosko guy?"

"Yes. He came upstairs to talk with us," Joe said.

"I didn't think to mention it before, but he checked in thirty seconds after Robert Parker checked in."

"You mean he was here before the murder?" Katie asked.

"That's right."

"That does seem suspicious," Connor said, "He said he was sent here. Either he was lying, or he was assigned to follow Parker, hoping he would lead him to the jewels."

"I think we need help on this," Katie said as she took out her phone. "I'm going to call Gabe."

"Who's Gabe?" Connor asked.

"He is a police captain in Milwaukee who is also our friend," Joe said.

Katie dialed the number and put the phone to her ear. Gabe answered and said, "Hello, Katie. Are you back home?"

"Sort of. We're at the resort. There's been a murder here."

"You're kidding?"

"Nope. We can't get away from it. I'm here with Joe and Detective Connor from the local sheriff's department. I'm going to put you on speaker."

Katie hit the speaker button, and Gabe said, "What can I do for you?"

"Hello, Captain. This is Detective Jennifer Connor. Do you have a Sergeant Jack Rosko under you?"

"No, but I know who he is. I met him a couple of times. I believe he is in District One. Why do you ask?"

"A man named Robert Parker was murdered here. He was accused of stealing jewels from your mayor. Are you familiar with that case?"

"I'm only familiar with what I've seen on the news. We had no part in that investigation here. How does that relate to Jack Rosko?"

"Well, Sergeant Rosko is here investigating the murder, but he arrived before Robert Parker was killed."

"Oh, that is suspicious."

"Can you speak with his captain and find out why he is really here?"

"I'll give him a call and let you know."

"Thank you so much, Captain."

"Thank you, Gabe," Katie said.

"By the way, Detective," Gabe said. "The two people with you right now are excellent investigators. Use them if you can, but please, keep them out of trouble."

"Thanks a lot, Gabe," Katie said, "but we don't need a babysitter."

"I'm not so sure."

They said their goodbyes, and Katie hung up the phone. She said, "He was joking."

"Which part?" Connor asked.

"We should probably eat too," Joe said, attempting to change the subject. "I'm hungry. Would you like to join us, Detective?"

"No, thank you," She said. "They will be moving the body soon, and we need to wrap this up."

Joe and Katie headed to the restaurant. They found everyone seated at a large round table. Two seats were empty, as if they were expecting them.

"Glad you could join us," Susan said. "It feels like Thanksgiving. Now we need Michael."

"We should meet like this more often," Joe said. "It shouldn't take a murder to bring us together."

"You're right," Sarah said. "We should make this a monthly ritual."

"That's a great idea," Joe said.

They ate and talked for half an hour before Eric went to the front desk, and Michael joined them for lunch. When they finished, Joe and Katie went to the crime scene, where they found Detective Connor and several deputies. "We'll be out of your hair in a few minutes," she said.

"What should we do about the room?" Joe asked.

"We finished what we needed to do here, so I recommend finding a cleaning crew specializing in this kind of work. She looked through several business cards and found the one she sought. "Here. These people do a good job." She took out another card. "You can reach me anytime at this number. Call me if you think of anything else that might help."

Katie took out one of her last remaining business cards from the television station. "Here," she said. "I don't work there anymore, but the phone number and email are still valid. Give me a call if you learn anything. I don't like knowing a murderer is running loose around here."

As they walked back to the lobby, Joe asked, "Do you think the killer is still here on the property?"

"Don't you? Wouldn't you stick around if you were the killer and didn't get what you were looking for?

When they reached the lobby, Michael and Eric were there. "Katie and I are going home," Joe said. "There's a small possibility the killer is still on the property. If he is, he's probably looking for the jewels like everyone else, so I doubt there is a danger, but you both should keep your eyes open and be careful."

Chapter 3

"It feels so good to be home," Katie said as she and Joe entered their house. She sat on the sofa, put her feet up, and said, "I just want to be a couch potato for the rest of the week."

Remembering what happened when they returned home from their honeymoon, Joe asked, "Do you think it's safe for me to bring the luggage in now?"

"If you're thinking about what happened last time, don't worry. I'm not answering the phone if someone calls with an emergency."

Joe raised an eyebrow. "How will you know whether or not it's an emergency before you answer?"

"I'll know," Katie assured him. "Now, stop complicating things with logic and go get our luggage."

Joe laughed, went outside to the car, and returned with their suitcases. He set them down and sat next to Katie. She put her head on his chest and asked, "Before you met me, how many murders were you involved with?"

"Directly? Let me think. One, two, three, four. Zero. The answer is zero, give or take zero."

Katie shook her head and looked at the ceiling. "So, it's me. I'm bad luck."

"You're not bad luck. How many murders were you involved in before meeting me?"

"I never even saw a dead body outside of a funeral home before that Williams couple."

Joe hugged her. "So, you see? You're not bad luck."

"Maybe the two of us together put out some kind of murder vibe."

"First, there is no such thing as a murder vibe. Second, none of those murders happened when we were nearby."

Katie sighed. "That may be true, but I'm starting to lose track of how many times someone almost killed us."

Joe hugged her tighter. "That is concerning, but the fact that we are both alive and well is encouraging. If a higher being is out there, perhaps he is looking out for us."

"Or she," Katie said

"Or she," Joe agreed.

Katie relaxed a bit. "You know what? You're right. If God sent a guardian angel to watch over us, we have nothing to worry about."

Perhaps, if Joe were part angel, a true angel could be protecting them. Of course, that didn't explain why the previous healers were killed. Under that logic, they would also have been part angel and under the protection of real angels. Even so, the possibility gave Katie some hope that they would always be able to overcome adversity.

Joe's expression turned serious. "Wait a minute. I didn't say we don't have to worry. We need to be cautious and stop taking risks. Especially now that you're pregnant."

"Joe, I have no desire to put myself or you in mortal danger again, but a life without risk is no life at all. Everything is risky. Just going to sleep puts us at risk of a home invader."

"I understand what you are saying, but you must still look before you leap. Risk can't be eliminated, but it can be reduced."

"Okay, I agree. I'll be careful. Now, can we feel the baby again?"

Joe smiled. "Certainly."

He held Katie's hand, closed his eyes, and concentrated. Soon, they were connected and could both feel everything. Katie ignored the rest of her body and focused on a tiny spot inside her. Despite its small size, its life force filled her with joy. "Can you tell if it's a boy or a girl yet?" Katie asked.

Joe concentrated for several seconds. "I'm afraid I have no experience with embryos. I can't tell what it is yet."

"I don't like that term 'it,'" Katie said. "Let's call her 'she' until we know more."

"Okay. I can't tell if she is a boy or a girl yet."

"That's okay. It doesn't matter. I'll be happy with either."

Katie's phone rang. "Oh, damn," she said and let go of Joe's hand. She couldn't reach her phone, so she got up and retrieved it from the coffee table. She sat next to Joe again and showed him it was Gabe calling.

"What if it's an emergency?" Joe asked.

"It's not," she said confidently. She answered and put it on speaker, "Hi, Gabe."

"Hi, Katie. I just wanted to let you know I spoke with Sergeant Rosko's captain. He says Rosko is on vacation."

"Really? That's interesting. Thanks for letting us know, Gabe."

"I don't know what's going on up there, but you two should give it a rest. Let that detective do her job."

"Are you worried about us, Gabe?" Katie asked.

"I feel like a father with two rebellious children."

"We'll be careful, Dad. Thanks for calling."

"Let me know if there's anything else I can do to help."

"We will. Thanks, Gabe."

When Katie hung up, she put her head back on Joe's chest. "Why do you think Rosko lied about why he is here?"

"I don't know. I would guess he has a personal vendetta against Parker. Maybe he felt his punishment wasn't strong enough and hoped to find him with the jewels so he could send him back to jail. The other possibility is that Rosko is a crooked cop who wants the jewels for himself."

"It can't be both. He would have to give up the jewels if he wanted Parker back in jail."

"Maybe not," Joe said. "If he wasn't too greedy, he could pocket some of the jewels and turn the rest in. He could claim that was all he could find."

"Do you think he killed Parker?"

"I don't know. It seems likely, but I hate to jump to conclusions."

Katie took out Detective Connor's business card and dialed her number. "Detective Connor. Can I help you?"

"Hi, Detective. This is Katie Novak. I have some news for you."

"You do? What is it?"

"I just spoke with Gabe, our friend in the Milwaukee Police Department. He says that Jack Rosko is on vacation."

"That's interesting, but I can't say I'm surprised. Thanks for letting me know. I have a feeling we opened up a can of worms, and his captain isn't too happy with him right now."

"No doubt," Katie said.

When Katie hung up, Joe said, "We did our part. Now, we should focus on getting back to our normal life."

"Yeah, yeah. Sure."

"With everything that has happened, buying this house, planning a wedding, getting married, going on a honeymoon, and saving Ashley, among other things, you haven't had a chance to start your job as marketing director. Tomorrow is Wednesday. I think it is an excellent day to begin."

"I'm sorry, Joe. You're right. I'll start working tomorrow, but tonight, I have a job for you." She leaned over and kissed him passionately. She pulled away and said, "You're on the clock starting now, and don't worry, I'm willing to pay overtime." She kissed him again.

Joe smiled. "I see you've already given me a raise."

Chapter 4

Joe woke up before Katie the following morning and made her a cup of coffee. He then poured himself a glass of orange juice and sat at the dining room table, flipping through a photography magazine that had arrived while they were in Milwaukee. Katie entered the dining room, stretched her arms, and sat beside Joe. "Thanks for the coffee. I need it," she said before taking a sip.

"Did you not sleep well?" Joe asked.

"I had a nightmare about Robertson. He was trying to inject me with poison, and you weren't there to stop him. Then I had trouble getting back to sleep."

Joe reached over and held her hand. "I'm sorry, Honey. I mean, Darling. Wounds that deep don't heal overnight."

"They do for you."

"I'm talking about psychological wounds."

"So am I," Katie said. "You don't seem affected by what happened."

Joe sighed. "I think men are better at hiding emotional pain than women are. It doesn't mean it's not there."

"Are you saying you are troubled by what happened, too?"

"Of course I am. When Robertson had us at gunpoint, I was terrified. Not for myself but for you and the baby. Even now, I get chills whenever I think about what might have happened."

"Exactly. That's how I feel."

"I think these feelings will diminish over time."

"I think they will diminish when I stop feeling like a victim."

"You feel like a victim? Don't forget we are here, alive and well and free, while the criminals we pursued are either dead or in jail."

"You're right. I just don't want to react to criminals anymore. I want them to react to us."

"That's the spirit," Joe said, squeezing her hand.

Katie's phone rang. She got up and retrieved it from the bedroom. Returning, she said, "It's Bob Martin."

"He probably heard about the murder," Joe said.

Katie answered the phone and put it on speaker. "Hi, Bob. What's up?"

"Hi, Katie. I just heard about the murder at your resort. Since it's a Milwaukee-related story, I need to get a reporter up there, and technically, you're still on the payroll until the end of the week. I'd like you to report it. I'll send Ashley up there with a camera."

"I think I'm done being an investigative reporter. Can't you send someone else?"

"I'm not asking you to investigate anything. Just report what you know."

"Katie sighed and said, "Very well. It's the least I can do for you."

"If you change your mind and want to investigate it, I will support you in any way I can."

"I don't know. I'll think about it."

After Katie hung up, she said, "It's my first day as marketing director, and I already have to report something that will hurt our business. Who will want to stay here with a murderer on the loose? It would be like booking a hotel on Amity after a shark attack."

Joe smiled. "A good marketing person knows how to turn something bad into something good. I know if you think about it, you will figure it out."

"Why do you have to be so cryptic? Can't you just tell me what you are... Oh, wait a minute. I know. Sometimes, Joe, you are a genius."

"I knew you would figure it out," Joe said.

They showered together, and then Joe made breakfast while Katie got ready. When the food was ready, Katie sat at the table, and Joe put a plate of bacon and eggs in front of her. He then added bacon and eggs to his plate and sat beside Katie.

Katie took a bite of the bacon and said, "This is perfect. Crispy, just like I like it."

"I know how you like a lot of things," Joe said.

"Yes, you do, but this is hardly the time to start that kind of talk."

"What kind of talk? I was referring to food."

"Okay. If you say so," Katie said, taking another bite of bacon.

"You seem chipper all of a sudden."

"Chipper? I don't think people use that term anymore."

Joe laughed.

What's so funny?" Katie asked.

I was just picturing you going back in time to when I was your age. You would need a translator."

"Times change, Joe. You need to keep up."

Joe got up and kissed Katie on the cheek. "That's what I have you for."

Katie slapped his arm as he picked up his empty glass. "I'm your wife, not your cultural liaison."

Joe laughed as he carried his glass into the kitchen and poured himself more orange juice. "You are my wife and my cultural liaison," Joe said while he was still out of reach.

After breakfast, Katie put on one of the sexy outfits that she wore as a news personality. It was a low-cut, tight-fitting teal dress. She completed the ensemble with a pair of sleek, black stilettos. She checked herself in the mirror and smiled.

Joe, a practical man who thought high heels were a stupid invention that only served to give women back issues, had to admit that Katie looked super hot. "Wow! Is this how you are planning to attract guests? I was thinking of something else, but maybe this will work even better."

"Very funny. You know very well that I'm dressed for television. You should put something nice on, too."

"Why? You'll be on television, not me."

"I want you to be there with me. We're a team. Besides, this story is about the resort, and I want people to see that this is a family-run business."

"Oh, I see. You have your marketing hat on. Okay. How nice should I dress? Do you want me to wear my funeral clothes?"

Katie rolled her eyes. "That would be better than what you are wearing now. Blue jeans and a flannel shirt make you look like a lumberjack. Come with me," she said, leading him to his closet.

She handed Joe a pair of tan slacks and a white, long-sleeved shirt. "You don't have much to choose from, but that should be good enough. We need to go shopping and buy you more clothes. Oh, and don't wear your sneakers today. Put on your good shoes."

"Yes, Mother."

Katie put her hand on Joe's cheek. "If your mother were still around, she would tell you the same thing."

"She probably would, which is why you reminded me of her."

"I think that's why men get married. They need someone to take over from their mothers."

Joe put his arms around Katie and kissed her. "I think men get married for a very different reason." He kissed her again.

The kissing became very passionate until Katie stopped and playfully pushed him away. "We don't have time for that now. Didn't you get enough last night?"

"Today is a new day."

***

Joe knew very little about computers, with two exceptions: He knew the resort's hotel management software and how to edit digital photos. Photography was his former profession and current hobby, so he had a desk in Michael's office that he mainly used to edit his photographs. Since meeting Katie, he hadn't gone out much to take pictures, but he planned on shooting more when things settled down. Now that Katie was working at the resort, Joe's desk was the perfect place for her to work.

Michael was at his desk when Katie came in. "Good morning, Katie. You look great this morning, but don't you think you are a little overdressed for the job?"

"Thank you, Michael. I'm dressed this way because I will be reporting the murder for my old news station today."

Michael sighed, "I was afraid the news people would get hold of this story. This could hurt business. Our slow season could become a no season."

"Don't worry, Michael. I have a plan."

"I don't know how you will make lemonade from these lemons, but good luck."

While Katie settled in, Joe joined Eric at the front desk. "You look good today, Grandpa," Eric said. "What's the occasion?"

"Katie is reporting the murder for her television station and wants to include me."

"I'm sorry," Eric said. "I know how much you hate attention."

Bill West approached and said, "Good morning. I'm looking for Jack Rosko. Can you tell me what room he is in?"

"I can't do that, but I can call him and let him know you are here," Joe said. "What's your name?"

He hesitated momentarily and said, "Bill West."

"Just a moment, Mr. West." Joe dialed a number and, when it was answered, said, "Good morning, Mr. Rosko. This is Joe at the front desk. Bill West is here to see you. He's in the lobby. Okay, I'll tell him."

Joe hung up the phone and said, "He will be down shortly."

Five minutes later, Jack Rosko showed up in the lobby. "What are you doing here, Bill?"

"Let's talk over here," Bill said, motioning for Jack to follow. He walked about ten feet away and stopped. "Cap knows you're here, and he's pissed."

"Shit! That damn detective must have called him," Jack said.

"I told you to leave it alone. How do you think it looks that an officer of the law follows a man after he does his time, only to have that man end up dead?"

Joe pretended to look at his computer screen but listened intently to their conversation. If Jack Rosco killed Robert Parker, maybe he would give himself away.

Jack's eyes narrowed. "Do you think I killed him?" he asked in a loud whisper.

"I don't know. Did you?"

"C'mon! You know me, Bill. Do you even need to ask that question?"

"I shouldn't need to ask you that, but you've been acting strange lately. Cap told me not to return without you, so pack your things."

"I'm not leaving."

"C'mon, Jack. Don't make this hard on me."

"I'm off duty. He can't tell me where I can or can't spend my time."

"He's gonna be pissed."

"What's he gonna do? Fire me for going to a resort on my vacation?"

"Probably not, but he can make your life hell. You could be riding a desk for the rest of your career."

"Those jewels are here somewhere, and I intend to find them. When I do, I can assure you I won't be riding a desk."

"If you find them, and that's a big if."

"I'm willing to risk it."

"Okay, fine. I'll help you, but only so I can get you out of here and return to work. Let's see if we can search Parker's room."

They walked back to the front desk. Eric was busy with a customer while Joe pretended to work at his computer. Bill West approached Joe, took out his badge, and said, We need to see the room the shooting victim was in yesterday."

Joe looked at the badge and said, "This isn't Milwaukee. You men are far from your jurisdiction."

"You're right," Bill said. "We have no authority here, but we hope you will help us out. It's very important."

Joe liked that he didn't try to bully him and said, "If you're looking for jewels, you should know that the sheriff's deputies already searched the room."

"We would still like to look for ourselves," Jack said. "Sometimes people miss things."

"Very well," Joe said, figuring that a fresh pair of eyes, or two, might see something the deputies had missed. He grabbed the key and led them to the room where Parker was shot. He opened the door, and they all went in. The crime scene cleaning crew had not yet arrived, so blood was still on the floor.

"Did the deputies open all these cabinets and drawers? Bill West asked.

"No," Joe said. "It was like this before they arrived, although I'm sure they searched the room again."

Jack looked at Bill and said, "Just like I thought. If the killer searched the entire room, he probably left empty-handed. That means the jewels are still here."

"I'm starting to think you are right," Bill said.

They both started to search the room. Joe just watched, thinking they were wasting their time, but hoping they would find something. After ten minutes, they both gave up. Bill said, "Where is the room Parker was in when he was arrested in November?"

"That room is upstairs," Joe said.

"Can we see that one?" Bill asked.

"Didn't you search it when you arrested him?"

"Yes, but if Parker returned here, that means we missed something."

"You should know that the Sheriff's Department also searched the room. It's doubtful you'll find anything."

"You never know," Bill said. "It's amazing what gets overlooked in an investigation."

Joe didn't have a master key, so he returned to the front desk and got the key to room 203. He led the men upstairs and unlocked the door. After entering, Bill and Jack immediately started searching the room. Joe just waited until they gave up. They looked at every conceivable hiding place. Finally, Bill looked at Jack and said, "There's nothing here."

"Well, it was worth a shot," Jack said.

"We appreciate you letting us look," Bill said. "If this room is available, I'd like to stay here for a night or two."

"Let's go back to the front desk, and I'll set you up," Joe said.

***

After checking Bill West in, Joe headed to the office expecting to find Katie immersed in her marketing work. Michael was busy with a guest, leaving Katie alone in the office. As Joe entered, Katie quickly closed the screen on her laptop. "Are you here to check up on me?" she asked, defensiveness in her voice.

"What are you hiding?" Joe asked as he reached over and flipped the screen back up. "This doesn't look like marketing."

"Okay, fine. You caught me. I was reading more about Robert Parker."

"You are quite the curious one, aren't you?"

"I'm sorry. I can't help it. It's in my blood."

"I want you to follow your passion," Joe said, "but I also want to keep you safe."

"I know you do, and I want that too. Perhaps we just ran into a streak of bad luck. I've been thinking. Plenty of people investigate murders for a living. Most of those people live a long time without ever being shot, blown up, or injected with poison."

"That's true. You may be right, but what if you're not?"

"As I said, everything you do in life is a risk."

Joe sighed and said, "Okay, tell me what you learned."

Katie's eyes lit up. "Well, he's thirty-eight years old and has been arrested several times. Most of the arrests happened when he was a minor or a young adult. He was finally sent to prison for three years for burglary when he was twenty-six. Another man named Jerome Lawrence was arrested with him and also sentenced to three years in prison. Jerome must have been a friend he grew up with. They are nearly the same age, and Jerome was arrested with Robert twice before they turned eighteen."

"What happened after he got out of prison?"

"It seems both he and Jerome went straight for a while. Either that or they became better criminals and didn't get caught. Robert got a job with a pest control company and worked there until he went to jail. I don't know what happened to Jerome."

"The name 'Jerome Lawrence' sounds familiar," Joe said.

"Maybe it's a common name."

"It probably is, but I think I either heard the name or read it recently."

"You mean since we've been back here?"

"Yes. I think I remember now. Follow me."

Joe led Katie to the front desk, where Michael and Eric stood. Michael had just finished helping a guest. "Have you heard the name 'Jerome Lawrence?'" Joe asked him.

"Yes. He checked in this morning. He calls himself 'Jay.' I think he might be connected to that Parker guy."

"Why do you say that?" Joe asked.

"Well, it was strange. They checked in one after another. First, it was Robert Parker who checked in. A minute or two later, Jack Rosko showed up. As soon as I checked him in, Jay Lawrence came in looking for a room."

"That might have been a coincidence. What makes you think they are connected?" Katie asked.

"They're connected because none of them had luggage. What are the odds of that being a coincidence?"

"You're right. They are connected," Joe said. "Lawrence and Parker were arrested together several times. We think they grew up together."

"Are you investigating this?" Michael asked. "I would think you two would want a break from that investigating stuff after what happened in Milwaukee."

"We just don't like having thieves and murderers here at the resort," Katie said, not believing her own words. "The sooner we find them, the better."

"I suppose you have a point," Michael said.

"Plus, I'm getting paid by the news station until the end of the week. I feel somewhat obligated to do something for that money." She also didn't believe those words. If she were honest with herself, it was the challenge she craved.

The door opened, and Ashley Taylor walked in. She looked much better than she did the week before when she was on death's door. She pushed her long blond hair back and smiled when she saw Katie and Joe. Katie walked around the desk and hugged her friend. "I'm so glad Mr. Martin sent you and not someone else," she said.

"I think he knows what we've been through together."

Katie turned and said, "I know you met Michael at our wedding."

"They shook hands, and Ashley said, "Of course. It's nice to see you again."

"What you don't know," Katie said, "is that Michael is Joe's grandson."

"You're his grandson?" Ashley said in disbelief. "That is so weird. You look more like his dad. No offense."

Michael looked at Joe and asked, "Have you told the whole world yet?"

"Relax," Joe said. "Ashley won't tell anyone. Besides, it was necessary to save her. You'll be happy to know that while I was away, I learned how to keep people from knowing my secret, and Ashley helped me practice on her. Now I can heal people without their knowledge."

"He's right," Ashley said. "It took a while, but he learned to block me out."

"You mean you can block people from feeling what you feel?"

"That's right," Joe said.

"It's amazing how far you have come since meeting Katie," Michael said.

Katie smiled, and Joe said, "I was fortunate she ran me over with her car that day."

Katie's smile disappeared, and she said, "I told you before I didn't run you over. I ran you under. If I had run you over, you wouldn't be here today."

"With that little car of yours. I'm not so sure."

Everyone but Katie laughed. She looked at Ashley, annoyed, and said, "Do you need help with your equipment? I'm sure Joe wouldn't mind."

"Not at all," Joe said.

"Okay. I guess I can use some help."

Joe looked at Katie and smiled as he followed Ashley outside. He knew Katie loved her little Mini Cooper and didn't like people making jokes about its size, so Joe took pleasure in teasing her about it now and then.

Joe also took pleasure in the weather. It was nearly perfect, cool enough to be refreshing but not so cool that he needed a jacket. Joe couldn't wait for things to settle down so he could go out and take pictures again.

They reached the news van, and Ashley slid open the side door. She handed Joe a large tripod. She climbed inside, opened a case, and removed her camera. Joe held the camera for her as she got out and closed the door. She took her camera from Joe, and they walked back to the front entrance. Joe stopped and said, "It's a little overcast today. I think the lighting is good for filming outside."

"I agree," Ashley said. She looked around and pointed to her right. "Let's set up over there. We can get a good shot of the front entrance."

They walked about ten paces before Joe opened the tripod and set it on the ground. Ashley put the camera on it and said, "Let Katie know we'll be shooting outside."

Joe went inside and told Katie, who asked Michael and Eric to join her. When they were all outside, Katie directed everyone on where to stand. "Okay, Ashley. Let me know when you are ready," she said.

Ashley held up three fingers and counted down. "Three, two, one, go."

"Hello, Milwaukee. This is Katie Novak reporting from Three Eagles Ski Resort in Waushara County. This may be my last report. As some of you know, I left the station in January and recently got married. Full disclosure: I now work as marketing director at this same resort."

She locked arms with Joe and said, "This is my husband, Joe Novak. Joe was my partner in the two murder investigations we recently conducted for Channel 23 news. His family owns and operates this lovely resort. Next to Joe is Michael Owens, who manages the resort, and his son Eric Owens. We're here to talk about a Milwaukee-related murder that happened here yesterday. You may remember Robert Parker, the man who was convicted of breaking into Mayor Ford's home back in November. He was released from jail yesterday and came here to the resort, the very place he was found and arrested after the break-in. He was shot and killed by an unknown assailant shortly after checking in."

Katie looked at Eric and said, "Eric. You heard the gunshot. Tell us what you did next." She held the microphone in front of Eric.

"Well, after confirming it wasn't a television turned up too loud, I knocked on the door. I heard no response, so I opened the door to investigate. I thought it might be a suicide attempt. When I saw the body lying on the floor, that confirmed my suspicion. At least I thought it did, but someone hit me from behind and knocked me out."

Katie held the microphone in front of Michael and asked, "What happened next?"

"I was at the front desk and got a call from someone who heard a gunshot. I hurried to investigate and found Eric unconscious next to the body. I was never so scared in my life, but to my great relief, he opened his eyes when I checked for a pulse."

"Thank you, Eric and Michael, for speaking with us today," Katie said. "Everyone here is happy you are okay, Eric."

She turned to the camera and said, "Robert Parker was accused of stealing $200,000 worth of jewels from Mayor Ford's home. The police never found the jewels, so Parker couldn't be charged with the theft. There is speculation, however, that he hid the jewels somewhere on this property. That may be why he returned here, and that may also be why he was killed. There is evidence to suggest the killer did not find the jewels, and the mystery remains a mystery. This is Katie Novak for Channel 23 news."

Katie handed the microphone to Ashley, and Michael said, "That was genius, Katie. I think you earned your marketing salary for the next month."

"Thanks, Michael, but Joe deserves some credit. He inspired the idea."

"You guys make a great team. It's good to see that again."

"Again? What do you mean by 'again?'" Katie asked.

"Oh, I'm sorry. I was referring to how well Pops and Grandma worked together. I hope that doesn't bother you."

Katie took Joe's hand and squeezed it. "I'm not bothered at all. I know Joe and Maria had a great relationship, and I'm happy that Joe was happy."

"I know it's a little early," Joe said, "but maybe we should eat lunch while Ashley is still here."

"That's a great idea," Katie said. "Would you like to join us for lunch, Ashley?"

"I'd love to. It may be a while before I see you guys again."

Joe looked at Michael, who said, "You guys go ahead. Eric and I will handle the front desk."

They returned Ashley's equipment to the news van, went to the restaurant, and were seated at a table near a window. In the winter, the window offered a great view of the ski slopes, but now, it was mostly dirt, with a couple of people on mountain bikes in the distance.

"This is a nice place you have here, Joe," Ashley said. "I am definitely coming back in the winter."

"Thank you, Ashley," Joe said. "We would be happy to see you any time of year."

"That's right," Katie said. "We're only a couple of hours away. You should come up with the family some weekend."

"I'm sure it won't be hard to talk John into it," Ashley said.

A waiter came by and took everyone's order. When he left, Joe asked, "So, how are you feeling now, Ashley?"

"I feel great thanks to you. I feel better than I've felt in years. I think you fixed more than that bullet wound."

"I told Katie I wanted to get you to a hundred percent, so I tried to do that."

"What about your Dad?" Katie asked. "How is he doing?"

"He's adjusting without Mom. I try to visit him more often because I know he is lonely. He seems happy when I am with him."

"It's difficult losing someone you love," Joe said. "He will never fully get over her loss, but he will find happiness again."

"Are you speaking from experience?"

Joe smiled at Katie and said, "I sure am."

They ate and talked for another thirty minutes. When everyone finished eating, Ashley said, "Well, I need to get back to the station. I'm so happy I got to see you guys again."

They left the restaurant and returned to the front desk, where they said their goodbyes. When Ashley left, Joe covered the front desk while Michael and Eric ate lunch. Katie returned to the office to work on marketing.

When Joe wasn't busy, he checked on her. "How's the marketing going?"

"Great. Just great."

"Did you learn any more about that Lawrence guy?"

"A little. After he got out of prison, he returned to work at his parents' bakery in Racine. There was even a write-up about him in the local paper when he became a master baker."

"Why do you think he's here now?" Joe asked.

37

"I don't know. If he had gone straight, I think he would have wanted to stay away from his old life. Maybe we can talk to him."

"That would be the easy thing to do, but as innkeepers, we can't be nosing around in the personal lives of our guests."

"We can't exactly investigate a murder on our property without talking to the guests."

"I'm still not so sure we should be. Why don't we let that detective handle the investigation?"

"Really? She hasn't even been back to the property since yesterday. Don't you think she would want to talk to people here?"

"They talked to several guests yesterday. I don't know what else she could do here. Besides, she is probably working on multiple cases at the same time."

"If that's true, that's all the more reason we should help."

"She's not Gabe. She might not like us interfering in her investigation."

"We wouldn't be interfering. Plus, what she doesn't know won't hurt her."

Joe considered it and said, "I have a feeling I'm going to regret this, but fine. We need to be super careful and stay together as much as possible."

"We always do."

Joe heard the main entrance door open and looked to see who had come in. "Speak of the devil. It's the detective."

Katie got up, and they met Detective Connor at the front desk. "Hi, Detective," Joe said. "Did you learn anything about our killer?"

"We got the autopsy report. Robert Parker died of a gunshot wound, which was no surprise. There was also no indication that he had been beaten or tortured."

"So, that means the killer probably never recovered the jewels," Katie said.

"That's what I believe, too," Detective Connor said.

"It makes no sense," Joe said. "Why would he kill Parker before getting the jewels, or at least learning where they were hidden?"

"That's the question of the day," Connor said.

"Maybe the killer wasn't here for the jewels," Katie said. "Maybe he was only here to kill Parker."

"That's a possibility," Connor said. "But why would he search the room if that was the case?"

"I don't know," Katie said. "Perhaps killing Parker was the priority, and recovering the jewels was secondary."

"So, why would anyone want to kill Parker?" Connor asked. "He's just a small-time crook. I can see someone making a priority out of finding the jewels but not murder."

"It does seem odd," Joe said. "Maybe the reason someone murdered him has nothing to do with the Jewels."

"If it's not related to the jewels, then we have no motive," Conner said.

"None that we know of yet," Joe said.

"Have you given any thought to what 'Number Three' might mean?" Conner asked.

Joe and Katie looked at each other. They both shook their heads, and Katie said, "We don't know."

"Okay. If you figure it out or if you learn anything useful, please let me know."

"Of course," Katie said.

When the detective left, Joe said, "I noticed you didn't say anything about Lawrence."

"I noticed you didn't either."

"I thought maybe we could talk to him first."

"I thought innkeepers don't talk to guests about their private affairs."

"You're right, Katie. We should get the detective's attention before she drives away and tell her about Lawrence."

"No. You were right the first time. Let's go talk to him."

Joe smiled. "As you wish."

Chapter 5

After Michael and Eric returned, Katie and Joe found Lawrence eating lunch at the restaurant. He sat alone near a window. They approached, and Katie said, "Hi, Mr. Lawrence. I'm Katie, and this is my husband, Joe. Joe's family owns this resort. Are you enjoying your time here?"

"Hi, Katie and Joe. You can call me 'Jay.' I think you have a wonderful place here, but I didn't come here for enjoyment."

"Do you mind if we join you?" Katie asked.

"Sure. Have a seat," he said.

They sat down, and Joe said, "Let's cut to the chase, Jay. We know you're an acquaintance, possibly a friend, of Robert Parker. Someone murdered him shortly after you checked in. That's quite a coincidence. We haven't mentioned your presence to the police yet because we want to hear what you have to say first."

Katie learned early on that Joe doesn't beat around the bush when talking to people. Sometimes, she wants to cringe when it happens, but more often than not, the direct approach works wonders.

Jay put his fork down, leaned back, and said, "I know it looks bad, but I didn't kill Bobby. He was my friend."

"So, why are you here?" Katie asked.

Jay sighed. "I'm here because I was a bad friend."

"A bad friend? I don't understand," Katie said.

"If I tell you, you have to promise not to tell anyone, especially the police."

Katie looked at Joe, who nodded. "Okay, we promise not to tell anyone, including the police."

"Well, Bobby didn't break into Timothy Ford's home alone. I was with him."

Katie looked surprised. "My station did a story on the crime, and there was no mention of another person involved."

"Your station? Are you a reporter?"

"Yes and no. I used to be a reporter for Channel 23 News. Technically, I am still employed with them for a short time, but I also work here at the resort."

"That's interesting. Sorry, I don't recognize you, but I don't usually watch the news. It's always bad news."

"That's exactly what I told her," Joe said.

"Can we get back to the story?" Katie asked, somewhat annoyed. "Why did you break into Ford's home? From what I read, it seemed like you had both gone straight. Why would you risk going back to prison?"

"I was reluctant at first, but Bobby was in trouble. His wife was pregnant with their first child, he was late on his mortgage payments, and his employer cut his hours. He needed money fast. He reasoned that Ford was a scumbag and stealing from him would be like stealing from Hitler."

"Hitler?" I've heard some rumors about Ford, but you can't compare him to Hitler," Katie said.

"No, you can't, but Bobby was angry with Ford. The company Bobby worked for did pest control for most of the buildings owned by the city. About a year after Ford took office, the city contracted with a new pest control company. The word is that the owner of the new company was a friend of Ford's father, and he donated a large sum of money to Ford's campaign."

"So, he blamed his loss of wages on Ford and thought Ford should pay for it," Joe said.

"That's right. Anyway, we studied their patterns. I learned about the type of alarm system they had and how to disable it. Bobby learned that Ford and his wife were going to a charity event downtown that night. Two minutes after we broke into the house, I was in the bedroom, and Bobby was in the living room, when someone came in through the front door."

"I think I see where this is going," Joe said.

"Yes. As you can imagine, we were separated and scared of getting caught. I could see Bobby behind the sofa from the bedroom door. He saw me and waved me away. He mouthed something I assumed was, 'Get out of here.' The bedroom had a sliding door that led to a deck, so I slipped out the door and never looked back."

"So why did Bobby end up here?" Joe asked. "Did you plan to meet here?"

"No. We didn't plan on getting caught. I have no idea why he came here."

"So why are you a bad friend?" Katie asked.

"Because he never told anyone I was with him, and I didn't have the courage to visit him in jail to thank him. At first, I wanted to tell him I was grateful to him for not mentioning me, but I couldn't voluntarily walk into a jail. I spent three years in prison and didn't ever want to be anywhere near a prison or a jail. Later, I wanted to apologize for not visiting him sooner, but I never got up the nerve."

"If that's the case, why risk another break-in where you could have been caught and sent back to jail?"

"I don't know. Part of me wanted to say no, but the other part said I couldn't abandon a friend in need. I guess that part won out."

"Why did you come here now?" Joe asked.

"Because I had no fear of visiting Bobby outside of a jailhouse. When I knew he was getting out, I went to his house but missed him by a couple of minutes. His wife told me he was coming here, so I came here too. I wanted to apologize, but I worried he would be angry with me. I decided to get a room. I needed time to practice what I would say to him. As soon as I settled into my room and practiced my speech, I went downstairs to see if I could find Bobby. I didn't want to ask for him directly. I was worried he would refuse to see me. I didn't make it very far before learning someone was shot. I later found out it was Bobby."

"What do you know about the stolen jewels?" Katie asked.

"Only what I heard on the news. I never saw any jewels. We weren't there long enough to look. If Bobby stole the jewels, he did it after I left, but I can't imagine how he would have pulled that off with two men in the house with him."

"Maybe he did pull it off. Maybe you came to get your cut of the jewels," Joe said.

"It's not like that," Jay said. "If the jewels are here, I want to find them for Stacy."

"Stacy?" Katie asked.

"Bobby's wife. She really needs the help."

Joe watched Jay's expression for several seconds before Katie spoke up. "Okay, we've taken up enough of your time. Thank you for talking to us, Jay. Enjoy the rest of your lunch."

"Don't forget this stays between us."

"Of course," Katie said.

"Do you believe any of that?" Joe asked Katie as they walked out of the restaurant.

"He did sound convincing."

"He convinced me, too, but I recently learned that I am not as good at reading people as I thought. I don't know if people are better liars today, or if I am getting worse at reading them."

"Don't beat yourself up about it, Joe. It's in your nature to trust people. That's a good thing. I mean, you don't want to let people scam you, but seeing the good in people is an attribute I admire in you. Since we started investigating crimes, we have encountered many more unscrupulous people than usual. You're not used to that."

"I suppose you're right. I need to be a little more skeptical in the future."

They reached the office and went inside. Michael was working at his desk. Katie sat at her desk and looked up at Joe. "I hate to see you change. Maybe you can raise your skepticism a notch, but only during an investigation."

"Okay. I can do that, but this is our last investigation. After this, we return to being a normal couple with normal jobs."

Katie was looking at her computer screen and said, "Okay. If you say so."

"You're just saying that to appease me, aren't you?"

"Yes. I mean, no. Wait. What are we talking about?"

"Never mind."

Michael stopped what he was doing, looked up at Joe, and said, "If you're looking for normal Pops, I'm afraid that ship sailed long ago."

***

A couple of hours later, Katie shut off her computer and walked past Michael, who was still busy with administrative work. She met Joe at the front desk as he finished up with a guest. When the guest left, Joe said, "That was our fourth last-minute guest, and I booked several more for tomorrow. A couple more guests, and we'll be full, which has never happened in the off-season."

"This must be what California was like during the Gold Rush."

"Do you know who made the most money during that time?" Joe asked.

"No, but I'm sure you do."

"It was the people who sold mining equipment."

"I bet the hotels did well, too."

"No doubt," Joe said.

"Are you ready for dinner?" Katie asked. "I'm getting hungry."

"We don't have much food in the house. We need to go shopping."

"Let's go out to eat. We can go shopping tomorrow or this weekend."

"Should we go to Gretchen's, or do you have somewhere else in mind?"

"No. Gretchen's is fine."

Gretchen's was a family restaurant in town, not far from the resort. The town was very small and had only one restaurant, not counting a fast food place on the road that led to the highway.

Joe and Katie were about to leave when a woman came in, pulling a small suitcase on wheels. She was in her mid-thirties with straight brown hair tied in a ponytail. She was also pregnant. Very pregnant. Joe thought she might give birth at any moment. She approached the front desk and said, "Hi. I don't suppose you have any rooms available?"

"You're in luck," Joe said. "We have two rooms left. I can give you room 202 on the second floor. The view is not the best. It overlooks the parking lot, but it's quiet."

"That will be fine," she said.

"I just need your driver's license and a credit card," Joe said.

The woman dug through her purse and pulled out her driver's license and a credit card. She handed them to Joe. Joe looked at the name on the Driver's license. "Stacy Parker. Are you related to Robert Parker?"

"Yes. He was my husband."

Katie looked shocked at the revelation and said, "Oh, I'm so sorry."

"Thank you," she said. "I'm here to arrange the return of his body to Milwaukee." She started to cry. "I have to pick up our car, too."

Joe handed her a tissue. She took it and wiped her eyes. "Thank you. It is so hard. My husband is dead, my baby is almost due, and I don't know where I will get the money to lay Bobby to rest." She wiped her eyes again.

"Did your husband not have life insurance?" Joe asked.

"Are you kidding? Life insurance is a luxury when you can't pay your mortgage."

"I'm sorry," Joe said. "I can't help you with that, but I can waive the room charge for a couple of days."

"That will be wonderful. Thank you so much. It will make a world of difference at a time like this."

"Do you mind if I ask why your husband came here without you?" Katie said.

"That is kind of personal, don't you think?" Stacy said.

"Yes, it is. I'm sorry. It's just that the person who killed your husband might still be here. Do you know who would want to hurt him?"

"I have an idea, but it isn't anything I want to talk about right now."

"It's okay," Joe said and handed her the key. "Do you need help with your bag?"

"No, thank you. I can get it from here."

As Katie and Joe walked to the car, Katie said, "That was a nice thing you did in there."

"I was glad I was in a position to help her."

They got in the car, buckled their seatbelts, and headed to the restaurant. "I feel bad for her. I wish there were more we could do," Katie said.

"You told me last week that we can't save the world."

"No, I said you can't save the world."

"Aren't we a team?" Joe asked.

"Of course we are. It's just that you want to help everyone. I just want to help this one person."

"How do you want to help her?"

"I don't know, but I choose to have faith that something will come up."

"You are very wise."

"I learned that from you. You were certain that fate would find a way to keep us together, and lo and behold, an apartment building blew up, and here we are."

Joe smiled. "That's the power of positive thinking."

***

Gretchen's was an old brick building with a steeply sloped roof designed to prevent too much snow from accumulating. There was no greeter. Instead, a sign directed them to seat themselves. Joe saw Bill West and Jack Rosko sitting at a table and walked towards them. "Hello, gentlemen," he said. "How goes the jewel search?"

"Oh, hi," Jack said. "Joe, is it?"

"Yes, and this is my wife, Katie."

They both stood and introduced themselves before sitting back down. "We gave up looking," Jack said. "We figured with all the people coming here, we would let them search for the jewels and wait until someone finds something."

"How will you know if someone finds something?" Katie asked.

"Most people would find it difficult to hide something like that," Bill said. "If we keep our eyes open, we will know."

"Well, I wish you luck," Joe said before he and Katie found an empty table and sat down."

A waitress soon came to their table. She was around fifty, with her blonde hair tied in a bun. She had a friendly smile. "Hi, Katie. Hi, Joe. Long time no see. Are you just getting back from your honeymoon?"

"Hi, Patty," Katie said. "We got home and then went to Milwaukee for a while because my friend was shot."

"Oh, my! I hope your friend is okay."

"She's okay now."

"That's good news. That's why I like living out in the country. People don't get shot around here."

Katie looked at Joe and then back at Patty. She suppressed a laugh, knowing it would be inappropriate. "No, it's pretty quiet around here."

Do you guys want your regular?"

Katie looked at Joe again, who nodded. "Sure. That will be fine."

When Patty left, Joe said, "You told me the news station still employs you until the end of the week. Does that mean you can still get help from that computer nerd, Billy?"

"That's right. I didn't think about that."

"Maybe you can ask him to dig up information on those two guys over there. I would also like to know more about Robert Parker and his wife, as well as Jay Lawrence and Timothy Ford."

"The mayor? Do you think he's involved?"

"I have no idea, but it wouldn't hurt to ask."

Katie took out her phone and typed a message to Billy. She included all the names Joe mentioned and hit send. "Okay, I sent it. Hopefully, he will have something for us later tomorrow."

Joe put his hand on Katie's and said, "Okay, now let's talk about something besides murders."

"What would you like to talk about?"

"Let's talk about how beautiful you are."

"It sounds like someone is in the mood. We've been married for over two weeks. I thought you would be slowing down by now."

"Are you kidding? I'm just getting started."

When they got home, they both quickly threw off their jackets and were on each other like horny eighteen-year-olds. They showered together and then went to bed after barely drying themselves. They made love for what seemed like hours before finally falling asleep in each other's arms.

Chapter 6

Katie and Joe woke up with the sun. Joe sat up in bed, stretched, and said, "Well, young lady. I think it is about time you got to work on marketing."

Katie smiled. "Look at you being all bossy today."

"Technically, I own the resort, so I am your boss."

"You need to rethink that. You gave up all your boss rights when you married me."

"That's not how it worked with my parents."

"Seriously? That was a hundred years ago, Joe. Besides, you put this place in your daughter's name, so Susan is our boss if you really want to get technical."

Joe laughed. "You would make a good lawyer, my dear."

"You are right, though. I have some ideas for this place that I'm eager to get started on. Anyway, there's not much we can do about finding that murderer until we get more information from Billy."

"Okay, then. I feel like we are going to have a productive day."

Joe got up and made coffee. He poured Katie a cup and brought it to her in the bedroom, where she was getting ready. He returned to the kitchen, poured himself a cup of orange juice, and started making breakfast. There wasn't much food left in the refrigerator, but he found a few eggs and some cheese and decided to make omelets. When they were ready, Katie joined him in the kitchen.

"Thank you for making breakfast, Honey. You are so good to me."

"I thought you didn't like that word anymore."

"I changed my mind. 'Honey' is a perfectly fine word, and I am not going to let that asshole Robertson ruin it for me."

"That's the spirit. I hope one omelet is enough. We're out of eggs now. We need to go shopping."

"One omelet is fine. As long as we're not out of coffee, we'll be okay."

"We have plenty of coffee, but I did use the last of the cream."

Katie groaned. "We need to go shopping today. I can't drink coffee without cream."

"I believe I said that."

LAST CHANCE

***

When Katie and Joe arrived at the resort, Eric was at the front desk helping a guest. Joe stayed with Eric while Katie went into the office. Michael was at his desk working. "Good morning, Michael," Katie said.

"Good morning, Katie. Do you know we are one hundred percent full today? That has never happened in the offseason before. Suggesting hidden jewels are on the property has brought out lots of treasure hunters."

"If there are jewels hidden here, maybe one of these bozos will find them."

I hope someone does, but not right away.

Katie sat at her desk and got to work. About a half hour later, Joe burst into the office. "We have an emergency! The pregnant woman we checked in yesterday is about to give birth. Michael, call 911. Katie, come with me. I need your help."

"Me? I don't know anything about delivering a baby."

"I don't either. That's why I need you."

Joe grabbed a master key, and they hurried to Stacy Parker's room. They skipped the elevator and raced up the stairs. They found Stacy lying on the bed when they entered her room. "Something's wrong," she said. "I can feel it."

Joe went to one side of the bed and Katie to the other. Katie held one hand while Joe held the other. Joe concentrated and soon could feel what was happening inside Stacy's body. He recently learned how to keep others from feeling the same thing that he feels and put that knowledge to use here. "The baby is turned the wrong way," he said.

"How do you know that?" Stacy asked before she was hit with a contraction. She cried out in pain.

Joe looked at Katie and said, "I don't know how to help her."

"Didn't you ever watch medical shows on television? You need to use your hands and turn the baby."

"I'm not a doctor. I don't know how to do that," Joe said, panic in his eyes.

"Relax and take a deep breath. I have faith in you. You need to use your hands and your gift at the same time."

Joe took a deep breath.

"Gift? What gift?" Stacy asked.

"Shhhh," Joe said. "I'm concentrating."

Joe put both hands on Stacy's stomach and connected with her. He could feel from the inside the pressure he was putting on her with his hands. He could feel the baby's position and knew exactly what effect the movement of his hands was having on him. The baby was a boy. He knew that without knowing how he knew. That gave him hope that he would soon know the sex of his own child.

"What's happening? Katie asked.

"I think it's working," Joe said. "The baby is moving." He looked at Katie and said, "Please, get some towels."

Katie raced to the bathroom while Stacy was hit with another contraction. Joe could feel her urge to push. "Breathe," he said. "Don't push yet. He's not ready."

"How did you know he's a boy?"

"Lucky guess," Joe said.

Joe continued to push on Stacy's stomach with his hands until he felt the baby was lined up correctly. Just then, Katie returned with the towels. "The baby is ready," Joe said. "Push when you have the urge."

Katie held Stacy's hand as she pushed. Soon, Joe could see the head. "You're doing good. Keep going."

When the head was out, Stacy screamed. The baby turned and slid the rest of the way out. Katie was there with a towel, and she helped wrap the baby before Joe set him on Stacy's chest, the umbilical cord still attached. She held the infant and cried. "He is so beautiful."

Two minutes later, the door opened, and Michael held it for two paramedics who rushed inside. Katie and Joe backed away to give the paramedics room. They stood near Michael, who said, "So, how does it feel to be midwives?"

"It was a breach baby, and Joe figured out how to turn him around," Katie said.

Michael put his hand on Joe's shoulder and said, 'I'm proud of you, Pops."

"It was Katie's idea. She was a big help."

"I'm proud of both of you," Michael said. "You two should go home and get cleaned up. Eric and I can handle things around here."

Joe looked at his hands and his clothes and said, "Yes, I could use a shower."

They waited until the paramedics finished. When they put Stacy on a gurney, they allowed her to hold her baby as they wheeled her out of the room.

Joe, Katie, and Michael were in the hallway. When she passed them, she said, "Stop!"

The paramedics stopped, and she looked at Joe. "What is your name?"

"My name's Joe," He put his arm around Katie and said, "This is my wife, Katie." He put his hand on Michael's arm, "And this is my dad, Michael."

"Thank you all for helping me. Is Joe your given name?"

"Actually, it's Josip."

"I want you to know that I am naming my baby Robert Josip Parker. I will never forget what you did. It was amazing."

"That is very nice of you," Joe said.

As they wheeled her away, Michael put his hand on Joe's shoulder but said nothing.

Chapter 7

When Joe and Katie got home, they immediately got in the shower together. They washed each other thoroughly. As Katie ran the sponge across Joe's chest, she looked for flaws. She didn't find any. She knew he was physically perfect, but sometimes she looked anyway. She hoped to find one flaw. Something that would prove he wasn't too good for her.

Joe noticed she was distracted. "Are you okay? What's wrong?"

"Nothing. Nothing's wrong. Why do you ask?"

"You were deep in thought. What were you thinking about?"

Katie shook her head. "I don't want to tell you. You'll think it's stupid."

"Honey, if something is bothering you, it can't be stupid."

After a pause, Katie said, "Okay, fine. I just think you're too perfect. I feel like you are out of my league. What if another woman comes along who is as perfect as you are?"

"You have nothing to worry about," Joe said and hugged her. He stepped back. "Have you looked in the mirror? Look at you. You are in the major leagues. You can't get any higher than that."

"I look good with your help. What if you decide to stop helping me? I will get old and wrinkled."

"You looked fantastic before I ever started helping you. I lived with my first wife until she was in her eighties, and I loved her wrinkles and all. If I were to lose my ability to heal you and you were to grow old, it wouldn't affect how I feel about you. Furthermore, I am far from perfect. Maybe I am at my peak physically, but mentally, I have a lot of room for improvement. Like today, for example. I didn't know what to do about that baby, but you kept your cool and talked me through it."

"Yeah. I guess you're right. You do need my help an awful lot. I might need to find a less needy man."

Joe reached down and tickled Katie. "You're asking for it, young lady."

Katie laughed and put her arms around Joe. She kissed him and said, "You're right. I am asking for it. So, are you going to give it to me?"

"Oh, I love it when you talk like that."

An hour later, as Katie was getting ready, her phone beeped, indicating she had a message. She picked it up and saw she had an email from Billy. "Billy sent us information on those people we asked about," She said.

She wanted to read it on a bigger screen, so she got her laptop and sat on the bed. Joe sat beside her as she found the email and opened the attachment. She started reading it to herself.

"What does it say?" Joe asked.

"It says Jonathan 'Jack' Rosko is married with two kids, both in college. His wife is a lawyer, and together, they claimed an income of a little over $200,000 last year. They own a home on the south side of Milwaukee, valued at approximately $420,000. It was recently paid off. They have almost $200,000 in their retirement accounts but only $4,000 in their bank account."

"They have two kids in college," Joe said. "I'm surprised they have that much available cash."

"Nothing jumps out at me as suspicious," Katie said.

"You said they recently paid off their mortgage. Did they make a large payment to do that?"

"It doesn't mention that. Maybe they had a fifteen-year mortgage or bought the house at a bargain price after the market collapsed. Maybe they didn't owe much and decided to pay it off."

"Or maybe someone paid him a large sum of money to do something illegal," Joe suggested.

"I suppose that's possible, too."

"Who's next on the list?"

"William West is divorced. He has two teenage children who live with their mother. He lives in a condo not too far from Jack West, which he bought five years ago after his divorce. It is valued at around $245,000. He owes $90,000. He recently bought a New Nissan Leaf for $39,000. He got $12,000 for his trade and paid the rest in cash. His retirement account is valued only at $9,500, and he has about $2,500 in the bank. He's not exactly rolling in money, except where did he get the cash to pay for his car?"

"Maybe that's why he's not rolling in money. Maybe the wife got most of his retirement money, or maybe he cashed it out to put a down payment on the house. He might have saved for the last five years and decided to splurge on a new car. Or, maybe he is on the take."

"Maybe nobody is on the take," Katie said. "Maybe Parker was killed by someone else."

"That's possible. Who else is on the list?"

"Jerome 'Jay' Lawrence has never been married. He lives in an apartment on the west side with his girlfriend. He has no kids, no retirement savings, and owns no real estate. He does, however, have almost $35,000 in his bank account."

"Now, that seems a little suspicious," Joe said.

"I agree, but considering he has no children and a girlfriend who helps with the bills, maybe he is able to save a lot of money. I mean, if you live conservatively, it's usually easy to save money."

"I suppose you're right about that," Joe said. "Kids can be expensive."

Katie looked at Joe, "Are you worried our child will be a financial burden?"

Joe looked surprised. "Of course not. You know I have plenty of money."

"I happen to know you have no money. You put this resort and all your investments in Susan's name."

"Do you not trust Susan?"

"Of course I trust Susan, but what if something happens to her?"

"It's all been arranged. Her will specifies that everything I gave her will come back to me if she dies before me. I will talk to her about adding you to the will in case I die first."

"I don't want to talk about you dying. Let's get back to the list."

"Okay, who's next?"

"Well, there's our victim and his wife. They've been married for five years. They bought a modest house together shortly after their wedding. They are currently three months behind on their mortgage payments. They also have over $10,000 in medical debt."

"Medical debt? What's that for?" Joe asked.

"I don't know. It doesn't say here. Medical records are hard to get."

"Nothing there helps us very much," Joe said. "Perhaps the murder was committed by someone else. It might be unrelated to the jewel theft."

"Perhaps. We should go see Stacy Parker. Maybe she can tell us something."

"I agree. Can you call Michael and tell him we won't return for a while?"

***

When Katie was ready, they headed to the hospital. They went inside, and a friendly volunteer directed them to room 221 on the second floor. They found Stacy alone in her room. The door was open, but Katie knocked on it anyway.

Stacy saw who it was and said, "Joe. Katie. Please come in."

"How are you feeling?" Katie asked.

"I feel like I just won a marathon. I'm tired, but I feel good. I only wish Bobby were here to see his son."

"What about your parents?" Katie asked.

"I haven't spoken to my parents since I was eighteen. They did not treat me well growing up. As soon as I was able, I left with the few things I had and never looked back."

"I'm sorry to hear that," Katie said. "What about Bobby's parents?"

"Bobby's dad died when he was a teenager, and he didn't have a good relationship with his mother. I think that's why we were initially attracted to each other. We had a lot in common. Anyway, Bobby's mother met a guy and moved to Florida about ten years ago. It's just little Bobby and me now."

"Where is little Bobby?" Joe asked.

"They brought him to the nursery a little while ago. They thought I needed to rest, and I couldn't argue with them."

"I hope we're not disturbing your sleep," Katie said. "If you'd like, we can come back later."

"No. You're fine. I couldn't sleep anyway. I'm too wound up."

"Do you mind talking to us about Bobby?"

"I suppose I owe it to you. Why do you want to know about Bobby?"

"It's a long story," Katie said. "I left my job as an investigative reporter at Channel 23 News in Milwaukee to get married and work at the resort. I went back to work temporarily to investigate the shooting of a friend and former coworker. Since I am technically still employed until the end of the week, my boss asked me to investigate Bobby's murder. Joe is my partner both in marriage and in investigations."

"Oh, so you're a television reporter? I thought you looked familiar. Now I know where I saw you. Did you two just get married?"

"Almost three weeks ago," Katie said.

"Well, Congratulations. I know how exciting it is to be a newlywed."

"Thank you," Katie said. "We are very happy together, but let's talk about you and Bobby. Do you know who would want to kill your husband?"

"My first guess would be Timothy Ford."

"The mayor? Why?" Katie asked. "Do you think he's angry about the jewel theft? I would think he would want Bobby alive until the jewels were found."

"You don't understand. Bobby didn't steal any jewels."

"What? What are you saying?" Joe asked.

"I didn't know Bobby was planning that heist. If I did, I would have talked him out of it. We were struggling so much. Bobby's employer cut his hours, and when I learned I was pregnant, I guess he felt too overwhelmed."

"What about the medical bills?" Joe asked.

"You know about that?"

"Yes, but we don't know what they were for."

"That was another contributing factor, I guess. Shortly before I learned I was pregnant, Bobby learned he had cancer."

"Cancer? What kind of cancer?" Katie asked.

"They called it 'Small Cell Lung Cancer.' It's somewhat rare and fast-growing. Bobby was always a smoker, and it caught up with him too quickly."

"Could they do nothing about it?" Katie asked.

"They could have tried chemotherapy, but the doctors said it was doubtful it would extend his life more than a year or so. He watched what chemo did to his father and wanted no part of it. I hate to say it, but getting shot might have saved him from a lot of suffering. I only wish he could have accomplished what he came here to do."

"What did he come here to do?" Joe asked.

"He wanted justice. He felt like a failure and thought this was his last chance to do something meaningful."

"What do you mean by justice?" Katie asked.

"I suppose I should back up. Bobby told me what happened at Ford's house. He said two men came home right after they broke in. His buddy Jay escaped through the bedroom, but Bobby hid behind the sofa. He told me the men were having a conversation about something illegal. He got out his phone and recorded the audio. When the men entered another room, Bobby tried to slip out the sliding glass door in the living room, but he caught his wristwatch on

56

the handle. The watch snapped off and made a noise when it hit the ground. He left the watch behind and ran, which was a bad choice because it had his fingerprint on it. He heard someone yelling at him, but he just kept running."

"Did he see the men?" Katie asked.

"No. He said he only heard them."

"How did he know Ford was one of the men?" Joe asked.

"It was Ford's house. Who else would it be?"

"What about the resort? How did he end up there?" Joe asked.

"When Bobby returned to his car, Jay wasn't there. He assumed he found his own way home. So, Bobby drove straight home. He told me what happened and said he needed to go away for a couple of days to lie low. If anyone asked, I was to say he was visiting his Aunt Margaret in St. Louis."

"Why didn't he go to see his Aunt Margaret?" Katie asked.

"Because he has no Aunt Margaret. He does have an Aunt Mary who lives near here. He decided to visit her for a couple of days. Unfortunately, when he got to her house, he saw she had company, so he kept driving. That's when he came upon the resort."

"So what were the two men discussing that was so bad?" Katie asked.

"I don't know. Bobby wouldn't tell me. He said it was safer for me if I didn't know."

"Did he say who the other man was, or what happened to the recording?" Katie asked.

"He didn't know who the other man was, but he learned later."

"So, who was it?" Joe asked.

"I don't know. He wouldn't tell me that either. He didn't want me to know. He thought if I knew, I would be in danger, which scared the hell out of me because that meant he was in danger."

"What about the recording?" Joe asked. "What happened to that?"

"His phone was confiscated when they took him into custody. I assume the mayor was able to make that recording disappear because nothing was ever said about it."

"Do you know how they found him so fast?" Joe asked.

"I don't know. Maybe they were able to track his phone. I'm sure when someone breaks into the mayor's house, it becomes a top priority for the police."

"Especially when that someone has incriminating evidence on him," Joe said.

"Yes. I'm sure that was a factor," Stacy said.

"How was he planning on making things right?" Katie asked. "Without the recording, what could he do?"

"He made a copy before they captured him. That's what he came here to retrieve."

"Oh, wow!" Katie said. "So all of this has nothing to do with jewels. If that's true, that means Ford lied about jewels being stolen."

"Probably," Stacy said, "unless Jay took them."

"We talked to Jay, and he made it sound like he left the house before they even had a chance to look for valuables. Assuming he told us the truth, why would Ford lie about missing jewels?" Katie asked.

"Insurance money," Joe said. "I would ask Billy if Ford received an insurance payoff."

"I guess that would motivate someone to lie, but if he did file a claim, it won't prove he is guilty of anything."

"I suppose it won't," Joe said, "but if the jewels weren't insured, it would mean he was probably telling the truth about someone stealing them, even if that someone wasn't Bobby."

"That makes sense," Katie said. She took out her phone and sent Billy a message asking for the information. She then turned to Stacy and said, "One last question. The last thing Bobby said was 'Number three.' Does that mean anything to you?"

Stacy shook her head and said, "No. I'm afraid not. Is it a room number?"

"No," Joe said. "Our room numbers are three digits."

"What else is numbered over there?" Stacy asked.

"Well, some of our rental equipment is numbered, but none of those are single digits either."

"That is a mystery then," she said.

They thanked Stacy for her time and said goodbye. When they left her room, Katie said, "Let's go see the baby."

A nurse passed by, and Katie stopped her and asked where the nursery was. "Follow me," she said. "I'm heading in that direction."

She led them past the nurses' station, turned right, and pointed to a door on the left. "Right in there," she said.

"Thanks so much," Katie said before she and Joe walked inside.

They were in a small room with a large window. The room had very subdued lighting, probably to prevent reflections in the glass. Several babies were positioned on the other side of the window so that observers could easily see them. Katie spotted little Robert Josip on the far left, pointed, and said, "There he is. Isn't he adorable?"

"He's a cute baby," Joe said.

"All babies are cute," Katie said.

Joe pointed to the right and said, "What about that one over there?"

To the right was an incubator with a baby inside. It looked like a tiny baby boy, but it was difficult to tell from their position. "Oh, my!" Katie said. "He's so little. He must have been born prematurely."

"I was born prematurely," Joe said. "My mother told me the doctor didn't expect me to survive."

"You must have had your healing abilities since you were an infant," Katie said, looking at Joe, who was staring intently at the baby. "I know what you are thinking, and you can't help this one. If you try, we will surely get arrested."

"There must be something I can do."

"We talked about this before. I thought you accepted the fact that you can only do so much."

"How is this different from your wanting to help Stacy?"

"It's different because I wouldn't get arrested for trying to help Stacy."

"I know you're right, but walking away is still difficult."

"I'm sure it is, but this baby is not fully developed. You would have to be here daily to help him grow. You can't commit that much time even if someone would let you in there."

"I guess you're right."

"Science has come a long way since you were a baby. I think the child has a better chance than you think."

"I hope you're right," Joe said.

Chapter 8

After leaving the hospital, they headed back to the resort. "We need to talk to that Lawrence guy again," Katie said.

"I agree. If what Stacy Parker says is true, it seems unlikely that he wouldn't know that the jewel story was fake."

Michael and Eric were at the front desk when they returned to the resort. Both were helping a guest. The place was busier than Joe had ever seen it in the spring. When Michael finished with his guest, he said, "You two had quite the morning. So, how's the mother and baby doing?"

"They're both doing great," Katie said.

"It's a shame your news station wasn't here this morning."

"That would have made a good story," Katie said, "But it looks like you already have your hands full."

"Yes, we do, but this will die down in a few days. If nobody finds those jewels soon, people will assume they are not here."

"I'm afraid it's starting to look like there never was a jewel theft," Joe said.

"Don't say that too loud," Michael said. "What makes you think that?"

"Stacy Parker told us," Joe said.

"She thinks he hid a recording somewhere at the resort of Timothy Ford talking to another man about something illegal," Katie added.

"If that's true, we're going to have a lot of disappointed guests."

"We need to ensure they are having a great time while they are here so they come back," Katie said.

"I agree," Michael said. "Do you have any ideas?"

"How about an ATV tour? I can lead it," Joe said.

"That's a great idea," Michael said. "Katie, can you get the word out?"

"Certainly. When should we do it?"

"I think tomorrow morning would be a good time," Joe said.

"That sounds perfect. Let's have lunch first and then talk to Lawrence. I'll work on the flyer for the tour after that."

Katie and Joe went to the resort's restaurant. When they got their food, Joe said, "We've been so busy lately that we haven't had a good home-cooked meal in weeks."

"Would you like to cook dinner tonight?" Katie asked.

"I think I would. After we promote the ATV tour, we can go shopping."

"Maybe you can make that Hungarian Goulash again. I liked that."

"If that's what you want, I'll be happy to make it, but I'll cut the onions this time and show you how to do it."

"I'll never live that down, will I?"

"At least now, if you cut yourself again, I'll be able to heal you."

"If only you could help with the pain."

"I can help with pain. The human body produces substances that are natural pain relievers. They don't work as well as drugs, but they are safer, and I have learned ways to increase their production when needed. It was how I was able to sleep after you hit me with your car."

"That's amazing, Joe. Is there anything you can't do?"

"I can't leap tall buildings in a single bound."

"Maybe not, but I bet Superman couldn't deliver a breech baby."

"I would think one would need to know how to do that to qualify for the 'super' label."

"I agree, SuperJoe."

When they finished lunch, they went to Jay Lawrence's room. Joe knocked, and they waited. After thirty seconds, he knocked again. "Mr. Lawrence. Jay," he said loudly. "It's Joe from the front desk."

After another thirty seconds, Katie said, "I guess he's not here."

"Let's go find him," Joe said.

After a brief search, they spotted Jay Lawrence on the veranda, leisurely sipping a cup of coffee. "Hello, Jay," Joe said. "Did you give up looking for those jewels?"

"I guess I did. I have no idea where he would have hidden them. I figured while I was here, I would try to enjoy myself. Despite all the people, it still feels peaceful here."

"Yes. It's a great place to unwind," Katie said. "Do you mind if we join you?"

"Have a seat," he said, extending his hand towards the empty chairs.

Joe and Katie sat down. Joe said, "Bobby's wife was here. She had her baby this morning."

"What? She was here? How is she? How's the baby?"

"They are both doing fine," Katie said. "We talked to her at the hospital, and she raised some interesting questions."

"Really? What did she say?"

"Before we get into that, I'm curious why you didn't go to see her after Bobby went to jail," Joe said. "I mean, she wasn't in jail. You had nothing to fear by going to see her. You could have told her what you wanted to tell Bobby, and she could have passed on the message."

"How do you know I didn't see her?"

"Because if you had, you would not have needed to get anything off your chest now. Plus, she would have told you what she told us this morning," Joe said.

"What did she tell you this morning?"

"You first," Joe said.

"You're right. I didn't see her. The truth is, she didn't like me that much. I couldn't blame her. She had a husband who was doing well, considering he was recently in prison. I had turned my life around, too, but she worried that if Bobby and I hung out together, we would return to our old ways. I wish I could say she was wrong."

"Did you hang out together?" Katie asked.

"Occasionally. Bobby wanted to maintain our friendship, but he also wanted to appease his wife. Sometimes, we would all get together, and Stacy would be cordial, but she was never overly friendly towards me. I thought if I went to see her, she would blame me for pulling Bobby back into his old life."

"Couldn't you explain to her that it was Bobby who pulled you in?" Katie asked.

"Put yourself in Stacy's shoes. Would you believe me?"

"I suppose not," Katie said.

"I also thought it would be better if she blamed me. She didn't like me anyway, so what was the use of making Bobby look bad?"

"That was very noble of you," Katie said.

"So, what was it Stacy told you today?"

"She said Bobby never stole anything from that house," Joe said. "She said either Ford was lying about stolen jewels or you took them."

"Me? I didn't take anything. I got out of there right away. Maybe she's wrong. Maybe Bobby took the jewels and didn't tell her."

"Why would he not tell his wife?" Katie asked.

"I don't know. Maybe he thought he could protect her that way. Maybe he figured the less she knew, the better."

"She said something else," Joe said. "She said the two men who walked in on you talked about something illegal. She said Bobby recorded the conversation on his phone. When the police arrested him, they confiscated his phone, and the recording was never made public. Someone made it disappear. According to Stacy, Bobby made a copy and hid it somewhere on this property. That's why he returned here. It was his last chance to do something good."

"What do you mean by 'last chance?'" Jay asked.

Katie looked at Joe and back at Jay. "Bobby was dying. He had terminal cancer."

Jay looked shocked. "Oh, my God! I didn't know. He never mentioned it to me."

"He probably didn't want pity," Katie said.

"I don't understand. If Bobby didn't steal the jewels, why would Ford say he did?"

"We don't know," Katie said. "He might have faked an insurance claim. We are waiting to find out if he received money from his insurance company."

"We need to know the truth," Joe said. "We are not the police, and what you tell us stays with us. Did you steal any jewels?"

"I swear to you, I took nothing from that house."

"We also had you checked out," Joe said. "You have $35,000 in your bank account. Where did that come from?"

"How the hell did you get that information?"

"We know someone very good at finding information," Katie said.

Bobby sipped his coffee and leaned back in his chair. "Okay, fine. My life is an open book. I did not steal anything to get that money. After getting out of prison, I lived with my parents and worked at their bakery. I saved every dollar I could and bought a beat-up '69 Corvette. My dad helped me restore it, but all the money for parts came out of my pocket. It took years, but we got that car in pristine shape."

"Did you sell it?" Joe asked.

"Yes. My girlfriend, Jill, and I recently decided to get married. She wants to buy a house and have a couple of kids. She says her biological clock is ticking. I wanted that, too, so I sold the car to get money for a down payment. We haven't found a house yet, but we're looking."

"Congratulations," Katie said.

"Thank you."

"Okay," Joe said. "Now that that's settled, let's assume Bobby hid a recording somewhere on this property. Before Bobby died, he said, 'Number three.' Does that mean anything to you?"

Jay thought briefly, shook his head, and said, "No. Nothing."

Katie looked at Joe and said, "Looking for jewels is one thing, but trying to find a memory card could be impossible, especially if it's one of those tiny ones."

"Wouldn't his phone save a copy of the recording to the cloud?" Jay asked.

"We wouldn't have access to that," Katie said. "Besides, whoever had his phone would also have had access to his cloud files. I'm sure they would have erased them."

"I wish I could help," Jay said, "but I have no idea where he might have hidden something like that."

"Thank you, anyway," Katie said. "Let us know if you think of anything useful."

Katie and Joe went back inside. Katie went to her desk and got busy designing a flyer while Joe hung out at the front desk and talked to Eric. After a while, he told Eric to take a break. Katie finished the flyer shortly after Eric returned. She printed them out, and she and Joe walked around the resort, putting one on each door.

When they finished, Joe said, "I didn't realize you were a talented designer. I'm impressed."

"You must be easily impressed," Katie said. "I took a design class in college years ago. I know the basics, but I'm far from talented."

"Never underestimate your abilities," Joe said. "It's good to be humble on the outside but be confident on the inside."

"I'll remember that," Katie said.

They started walking back to the front desk when Katie's phone dinged. She looked at it and said, "I got an email from Billy."

"What does it say?" Joe asked.

"Just a minute," Katie said as she opened the message. "It says Ford did not collect any insurance money for the missing jewels."

"That's surprising," Joe said. "If it wasn't to collect the insurance, why would he lie about stolen Jewels?"

"I don't know. Maybe it's not a lie."

"Do you think Stacy or Jay are lying?"

"I don't think anything, but it's possible. It's also possible Bobby lied to Stacy."

"It feels like we just took a step backward," Joe said.

***

They worked for another hour, and then Joe said, "I think we need to go and pick up a few groceries so we can have a nice home-cooked meal tonight."

"I look forward to that," Katie said.

The nearest supermarket was thirty minutes away, so they decided to go to a local deli that also served as a general store. They picked up what they needed to make the Hungarian goulash and a few other essentials and then headed home.

Joe started cooking dinner while Katie watched him. The last time he made this meal, she tried to help him, but she cut her finger while chopping onions. That was at a time before Joe learned how to heal other people, but even knowing that Joe could heal her now if she cut herself again, she decided it was better not to risk it. Besides, her husband cooking for her was somewhat romantic.

After Joe sauteed the beef, he added the rest of the ingredients and set the stove to simmer. "Okay, this needs to cook for ninety minutes."

"Do you remember what we did last time while this dish was cooking?" Katie asked.

"I sure do. Do you think we should do it again?"

"I'm thinking we should make it a tradition."

"I like the way you think, young lady," Joe said and held out his hand.

Katie took his hand, and he led her to the bedroom.

When the food was ready, they ate it at the dining room table. When Katie left Milwaukee to be with Joe, she embraced some of his idiosyncrasies, including living without a television. Despite working as a television news reporter since she graduated from college, she thought not having a television might be good for her. She didn't want to be one of those couples who watched television until they were too tired for sex and then went to bed. Before meeting Joe, she had a habit of eating while watching television, but now she enjoyed having an intimate meal with her husband at the table without any distractions.

"This is delicious as usual," Katie said. "You could have been a chef."

"I do like to cook, but I wouldn't have traded my photography career to be a chef."

"I don't blame you. You got to see so many cool places and interesting animals. Is that how you ended up here? You told me you and your wife bought this place back in the eighties, but you never told me how that happened."

"That's a long story," Joe said.

"I'm not going anywhere."

"Well, we lived in Brooklyn until shortly after Susan was born. I was tired of living in the city and wanted someplace quieter, so we bought a house in a small town about forty miles north. I had returned from the war about a year earlier and was starting to make decent money with my photography. I enjoyed the simpler life in a small town, but I learned from some of my photo shoots that I was happiest in the wilderness surrounded by nature."

"I noticed that," Katie said. "It's funny that you started as a city boy and ended up here."

"I told you that my wife and I went through a traveling phase in the seventies. I didn't tell you how that ended. We stayed at a campground about ten miles from here. Someone had posted a flyer there for a cabin that was for sale. We went and looked at it and decided to buy it. We sold the motorhome and used the money to buy the cabin. We spent the summers in that cabin. I think it was near the end of our stay in 1982 that we learned the resort was for sale. It took a lot of wrangling, but since all our kids were married and out of the house by then, we ended up selling our home in New York and using that money and the money we had saved to buy the resort. Of course, we also had to borrow money, but it was worth it."

"So, how did Susan and Michael end up here?"

"The following year, Susan's husband died in a car accident. Susan was a housewife raising three kids and couldn't go out and get a job, so she came to live with us. We gave her the innkeeper's house, and Marie and I lived in the cabin. Susan worked at the resort for years while she raised those kids."

"Just so you know, nobody uses 'housewife' anymore," Katie said.

"They don't? Why not?"

"They call them 'stay-at-home-moms' now. I guess it's less condescending."

"I can't keep up with all these name changes," Joe said. "Some words that used to be euphemisms are now considered bad."

"Times change, Joe."

"The only constant is change," Joe said.

"Like this case that we're working on. I thought we were getting somewhere, but now Ford seems less scummy than we thought."

"I think we need to consider that the killer is no longer on the property, and we may never know who it was."

"I suppose that could be the case," Katie said. "Do you want to quit already?"

"I don't know. Maybe. It would be nice to return to a somewhat normal life and focus on the resort for a change."

Katie sighed and said, "I suppose you're right. It was probably stupid to get involved after what we've been through."

"It wasn't stupid. We found two murderers. That's quite an accomplishment for amateurs, but three for three is probably too much to ask for. I mean, I'd love to catch this killer, but maybe it's time for us to do our jobs and let the police do their jobs."

"You're probably right, Joe. Tomorrow, let's focus all our energy on the resort."

Chapter 9

Katie and Joe started work early the next morning. Several people signed up for the ATV tour, and Joe had to prepare everything. They arrived before Michael and Eric. A woman from the night shift was at the front desk. "Good morning, Lily," Katie said as they approached her.

"Good morning, Katie. Good morning, Joe."

"How's it going?" Joe asked.

"Good. A couple more people signed up for the tour last night," she said, handing Joe a printout.

He glanced at it and nodded, "Thanks."

They went into the office, and Katie sat at her desk. "Would you like to join us?" Joe asked.

"No, thank you. I've never driven one of those, and I'd rather not embarrass myself in front of a bunch of people."

"It's not that hard, but if you want, I can give you a private lesson another time."

"Yes. That would be nice. Make sure it's very private," she said, smiling.

As Joe gassed up the ATVs, Eric came to check on him. "Good morning, Grandpa. Can you use some help?"

"I would love it if you could come along and ride behind everyone in case of any issues."

"That sounds like fun. Let me check with Dad and make sure he doesn't need me." A few minutes later, Eric returned and gave Joe a thumbs-up.

Eight guests were on the list: three men, three women, and two teenage boys. When everyone was present, Joe took them outside and reviewed the safety instructions. He also told them beforehand what to expect since it would be too noisy to speak while riding. Joe brought along his camera and slung it over his shoulder. They all got on their ATVs and followed Joe.

He stopped at several places where the view was noteworthy. When they reached the highest point, they all got off, and Joe led them to a clearing where they could look out at the resort. Everyone took pictures, and Joe said, "I want to show you one more thing before we return. In my opinion, it is the highlight of this tour. For this, we need to walk. Follow me."

Joe led them back to the trail and then walked about twenty yards to another small clearing. "We need to be quiet here," he said, pointing ahead and to the right. "Do you see it?"

The guests gave a lot of "oohs" and "ahs" while they all took out their phones or cameras to take pictures. Joe snapped a few photos as well. They were looking at a bald eagle's nest less than twenty-five yards away. They were standing slightly higher than the nest, so they had a unique view inside of it.

One of the eagles sat guard on a branch above the nest, while the other perched on the edge of the nest, watching over the two eaglets. "The young ones were born about a month ago," Joe said. "Back then, these guys were small and fluffy. Now you can see they are pretty big and getting their juvenile feathers."

"When will they leave the nest?" one of the boys asked.

"They will probably be here for another six or seven weeks," Joe said.

They watched the eagles for several more minutes before returning to the resort. After saying goodbye to the guests, Joe and Eric returned the ATVs to the garage.

When Joe entered the office, Michael asked, "How did the tour go?"

"Very well. Everyone was impressed by the eaglets."

Katie stopped what she was doing and looked up, surprised. "Eaglets? You didn't say there would be eaglets on the tour."

"You made it very clear that you didn't want to risk embarrassing yourself, even though you told me the other day that risk was a part of life."

Katie made a pouty face, and Joe said, "They will be there for a while yet. I'll take you up there the next chance we get."

"You better," Katie said.

Joe removed his camera from his shoulder, took out the memory card, and placed the camera in the cabinet opposite Katie's desk. The desk used to be where he worked on his photos, but now he needed to work elsewhere. "I'm going to look at my photos," Joe said.

"Have fun," Katie said. "Oh, if you have any good photos, let me have a few, and I'll post them on our social media pages."

Joe looked surprised. "Since when do we have social media pages?" Joe asked.

"Since I became marketing director. You didn't hire me for my good looks, did you?"

"Well..."

Katie crumpled up a piece of paper and threw it at Joe.

Joe kissed Katie on the cheek. "I'm just kidding, Honey. You are the most capable person I know."

"I hope you don't forget that," Katie said.

Joe left the office and walked across the lobby to a door marked "Business Center." He opened it and saw no one inside. There was a printer to the right and three workstations against the wall to the left. A divider separated each one. Eric, the resort's unofficial computer guru, had replaced the aging computers a year earlier. The new computers were tiny, about the size of a small alarm clock. Joe remembered reading about computers after the war that were the size of entire rooms. The computers in front of him were millions of times more powerful than those computers and probably millions of times cheaper as well. It was a modern wonder that young people couldn't appreciate.

Joe was about to insert his memory card into the computer when he noticed the label stuck on it. It read "1." He looked at the computer to his right and saw it was labeled "2." His heart skipped a beat. He sprang from his chair and checked the far computer. Its label read "3."

Joe put the memory card in his pocket and hurried back to the office. Michael was busy with a guest, so he stuck his head in the door and whispered loudly, "I know what 'Number three' means!"

"You do? What is it?" Katie asked, standing up and walking to Joe.

"Follow me," he said

Katie got up and followed Joe to the business center. Once inside, Joe pointed to the label on the third computer and said, "Number three."

Katie's mouth hung open. "Oh, my God. He copied his recording onto that computer." Katie sat down and looked through the computer files. She checked the download folder but found nothing. She then looked in the documents folder, the desktop folder, and even the music folder. She didn't find any audio files. "I think we need Eric's help."

"I'll find him," Joe said.

Eric wore many hats at the resort, so finding him wasn't always easy. Instead of wasting time looking, Joe paged him over the intercom. Two minutes later, Eric showed up at the front desk, and Joe told him he needed help in the business center. When they arrived, they found the room empty and the number three computer missing.

Joe's heart sank. He stepped out of the room and looked both ways. "Katie!" He yelled. "Katie!"

He looked back at Eric, "Katie's in trouble. Call 911."

Joe went left and then turned left again, hoping to see her in the hallway. Eric raced to the front desk. Michael was still with a guest, but Eric interrupted him. "Katie's in trouble. I think she's been kidnapped. Call the police. I'm going to look for her."

The guest had a shocked look on his face. All Michael could do was say, "Excuse me," before picking up the phone and dialing 911.

Joe reached the back door and looked outside. Not seeing Katie, he raced back to the front door and went outside. He saw a car pull out of the parking lot and turn right. He had no idea if Katie was in that car. He went to the front desk, where Michael had just hung up the phone. The guest was still standing there. "The police are on the way," he said.

Eric returned to the front desk, out of breath. He looked at Joe and just shook his head.

"Dammit!" Joe said. "It's my fault. I should have stayed with her."

"There's no way you could have known, Pops," Michael said.

"We need to find her fast."

"Why would anyone kidnap Katie?" Eric asked.

"They must have overheard us talking about the recording. They didn't want her. They wanted to destroy that recording before anyone heard it."

"What recording? Eric asked. "What did I miss?"

"Robert Parker never stole any jewels. He had a recording on his phone of Mayor Ford and another man talking about doing something illegal. He downloaded that recording onto one of our computers. Specifically, computer number three."

"Oh, so that's what he meant by 'Number three.'"

"Exactly. Now the killer has the computer and Katie."

"What use is Katie to him?" Michael asked.

"I don't know. Maybe she saw his face and could identify him. Shooting her would have drawn immediate attention to him."

"I hope that's not true," Eric said. "Maybe he needs her for something."

71

Joe held his stomach and said, "I don't feel so good."

Michael came around the counter and helped Joe to a chair by the window. "Sit down, Pops," he said.

Joe sat down, and Eric said, "I've never seen you sick before, Grandpa."

Michael looked at Eric and said, "It's stress. Give him a minute."

Joe took a couple of deep breaths and stood up. "I'm fine," he said. "I can't sit here and do nothing while Katie's life is in danger."

***

Ten seconds after Joe left Katie to look for Eric, she felt the presence of someone standing in the doorway. She assumed Joe had forgotten something. When she turned to look, she saw a man wearing a baseball cap, dark sunglasses, and a mask. A person wearing a mask was no longer unusual, but what was unusual was a person wearing a mask while pointing a gun. At least, it was unusual for most people. Katie was all too familiar with it, and it was something she definitely did not like. "What the hell?" she said.

"Keep quiet, and you might live," the man said in a husky voice. "Now, pull all the plugs out of that computer and hand it to me."

Katie slowly reached over and started pulling out plugs.

"Hurry up!" The man snapped, his voice low but stern.

Katie pulled out the last plug and picked up the computer. She considered throwing it at the man to distract him, but he blocked her only means of escape. Instead, she handed the computer to him. He took it in his left hand and then put his gun in his right pocket, but kept his hand on it. "We are going to walk outside, and you are not going to cause a fuss. Do you understand?"

Katie nodded.

"Good. Now, let's go."

No one was in sight when they left the business center. The man motioned for Katie to walk toward a side exit away from the front desk. When they reached the parking lot, the man directed her through a group of cars and said, "Stop."

Katie stopped, and the man took off his cap, placed it over Katie's head backward, and positioned it so it covered her eyes. He grabbed her left arm and led her past a few more cars. He opened the passenger door. "Get in, and don't touch the cap. If you see me or my car, I will be forced to kill you. I don't want to have to do that, and I'm sure you don't want me to. So, can I count on you to be a good girl?"

Katie nodded slowly.

"Good. I knew you'd be agreeable."

Katie slid into the passenger's seat, careful not to let the hat move. The man slid into the driver's seat, and they drove away.

After driving for a couple of minutes, Katie figured asking the man a question wouldn't worsen the situation. "What do you want with the computer?"

"The same thing you want."

"What makes you think there is anything of value on it?"

"Sometimes, if you want to learn something, the best thing to do is keep your mouth shut and your eyes and ears open."

The man stopped the car and rolled down Katie's window. He said, "Get out very carefully."

Katie got out and stood next to the car. She wasn't sure if her situation had just gotten better or worse. Was he going to shoot her and leave her on the side of the road? Why would he do that after carefully hiding his identity? She couldn't discount the crazy factor, but this man did not seem crazy.

"Close the door and walk straight ahead."

Katie started walking. When she approached the treeline, the man yelled, "A little to the right." Katie turned slightly right and walked into the woods. After a few steps, she walked into a large tree. She lifted the hat but feared looking back. After hearing nothing for ten seconds, she turned around and saw an empty street.

She walked back to the road. To her right, the road turned sharply to the right, which was probably why he chose to drop her there. He could quickly disappear around the corner. She started walking back to the resort. She did come to appreciate the area's natural beauty and liked the slower pace, but now she wanted to see some traffic. Unfortunately, there wasn't a car in sight.

Chapter 10

Joe stood up from the chair and walked outside. Eric followed him while Michael returned to his guest. Joe looked out at the parking lot and tried to imagine how he would continue without Katie in his life. He lived alone for so long after his wife died. He was so addicted to her that when he lost her, he somehow lost himself. He never wanted to feel that pain again, so he shut himself off to new relationships until Katie came along. Now, he might have to go through the same emotional trauma again.

He then saw a police car turn into the parking lot. They drove up to the front entrance and stopped. Two sheriff's deputies got out and approached Joe and Eric.

"Did you report a missing person?" one of them asked.

"She's not missing. Someone took her," Joe said.

"Are you saying someone kidnapped her? How do you know?"

"Yes! Someone kidnapped her. I know because she and I just uncovered evidence related to the murder that happened here the other day. I left the room to find my brother, and when we returned, she was missing along with the computer that had the evidence."

They all went back inside, and Joe gave the officers a description of Katie. When he finished, the door opened, and Detective Connor walked in with Katie at her side. Joe raced over and hugged her. "I'm so happy you're okay. I was so worried. What happened?"

"I found her on the road, Connor said. "Whoever kidnapped her, let her go."

Joe kissed Katie and said, "I'm sticking to you like glue from now on. Tell me what happened?"

Tears formed in Katie's eyes. "A man with a gun came in after you left. He took the computer and made me go with him."

Joe hugged her again. "I'm so sorry. I never should have left you alone in there."

"You have nothing to be sorry for. How could you know?"

"Who was it? What did he look like?"

"I don't know. He wore a hat and sunglasses. He also had one of those medical masks on."

"What was he driving?"

"I don't know. He covered my face with his hat. He told me he would kill me if I took it off. Honestly, I didn't want to know who he was at the time. I didn't want to give him a reason to pull the trigger."

Tears rolled down Katie's face more heavily, and Joe hugged her again. "You did the right thing."

"She was smart enough to keep the man's hat," Connor said. "Maybe we can get DNA from it."

"How long will that take?" Joe asked.

"Probably two or three days if we put a rush on it, although it could be longer. Even then, it won't help unless the kidnapper is in the DNA database. It's too bad you don't have cameras here."

Joe looked at Eric and said, "Please, find someone who installs security systems. I don't care what it costs. We need cameras in here."

"Certainly, Gra . . . uh, Joe," Eric said before walking away.

"You really have a lot of influence around here," Connor said.

"Well, I guess he looks up to his older brother."

"You're older than Eric? I would have guessed he was older than you."

"You would have guessed wrong," Joe said.

"You look so young. You must have good genes."

"That's the understatement of the century," Katie said.

"So, what happens now?" Joe asked, trying to change the subject. "What will you do to find this guy?"

"I won't lie to you. It won't be easy to find him. Katie told me what happened. The guy is smart. He was careful not to touch anything, which makes looking for fingerprints a waste of time."

Michael finished with his guest and rejoined the group. Joe put a hand on his shoulder and said, "I think Katie's been through enough today. I'm going to take her home."

"Of course. Will you be in tomorrow?"

"I'm fine, Michael," Katie said. "We'll be here."

"Thank you for your time, Detective," Joe said. "Please let us know if you learn anything."

Joe took Katie's hand, and they walked outside. "Do you mind if we walk home?" he asked. "I can use the air."

"Are you okay?" Katie asked. "I was the one kidnapped, but you look pale."

"I'm fine," Joe said. "I just thought I lost you. It felt like my intestines were turned inside out. It wasn't a good feeling."

Katie stopped walking and pulled Joe toward her. They hugged for a long moment, and she said, "It sounds like you were more scared than I was. You can't lose me that easily. I'm afraid you're stuck with me."

"I can think of worse fates."

They continued walking, and Joe asked, "Are you saying you weren't scared?"

Katie thought for a moment, "Not like the last time someone had a gun on me. I mean, I was scared at first, but then I realized he went out of his way to disguise his identity. If he planned to shoot me, he wouldn't have bothered to do that. At least, that's what I hoped. I will admit that when he told me to get out of the car, I wasn't sure what to expect."

"I don't like the idea of carrying a gun, but maybe we should consider getting one for you," Joe said.

"No. I don't think I'm ready for that yet."

"What about a self-defense class?"

"That is something I would be willing to learn. Can you teach me?"

"Well, I had training in hand-to-hand combat in the army, but that was over eighty years ago. A lot of it has stayed with me, but I'm unsure if I would be a good teacher. We should find a professional."

"Okay, but only if you take the class with me."

"I wouldn't have it any other way."

They turned down a narrow road which was lined with trees on both sides. It was the road Katie was driving on during a major snowstorm the day she met Joe. Her GPS malfunctioned and brought her the wrong way. While trying to get her bearings, she hit Joe with her car. She stopped walking at almost the exact place where it happened. "There's a car at your cabin," she said.

"Yes. Michael started renting it out weekly."

Katie frowned. "Oh, I see."

"You seem disappointed."

"Maybe I am a little. It's just that the cabin holds a lot of good memories. It's where I got to know you. It's where I learned your secret. It's where we first made love."

"It has no bathroom. I thought you wanted a place with a bathroom."

"I do, and I'm happy with our house, but sometimes I think spending the night there again would be nice. I would like to repeat our first night together."

"I don't think you mean our first night together when I was recovering from you hitting me with your car."

"No, I mean our first night together," Katie said, stressing the word "together."

"I'll talk to Michael and reserve it for us as soon as it is available."

They started walking again, and Katie said, "I couldn't ask for a better partner."

"The feeling is mutual," Joe said.

When they reached their house, Joe opened the door and held it until Katie walked inside. He followed her in and closed the door. Katie sat on the sofa and put her feet on the coffee table. Joe sat beside her, and Katie put her head on Joe's chest. "Well, our life isn't boring. I guess I don't have to worry about that."

"No, it's not," Joe said. "Sometimes it feels like we are on a rollercoaster."

"Your analogy is exactly right. It has been both scary and exhilarating."

"Did you really find getting kidnapped to be exhilarating?"

"I think that mainly falls into the scary category, but yes, there was something exhilarating about it as well. I know it sounds crazy, but you become laser-focused when your life is in danger. The past and the future fade away, and you live in the moment. I'm not suggesting we put ourselves in danger, but I like the feeling of living in the moment."

"I totally understand. Many ancient philosophies and religions teach about living in the moment, like Buddhism and Taoism. Even Jesus taught about it."

"You always impress me with how much you know."

"If you don't watch television, you have plenty of time for reading."

"I hope that's not a dig at my life before I met you. We don't have a television now, and I am perfectly happy without it."

"I would never criticize your former life. It made you who you are today, and I couldn't be happier with that person."

Katie turned and kissed Joe, "I couldn't be happier with you, too. Now, do you think we can feel the baby again? When you felt that other woman's baby, you knew it was a boy. Maybe you can tell with our baby now."

"I'll try," Joe said and connected with Katie. They could both feel the baby inside Katie. Joe tried to remember how he knew the baby was a boy. He didn't know it because of the baby's physical appearance. He seemed to know it on a deeper level. He just knew he was a boy without knowing why. He concentrated intensely on Katie's baby but could not achieve that same level of knowing. The baby was too young and not developed enough."

"I'm sorry, Honey. I just can't tell yet."

"That's okay," Katie said. "I know she's still too young. We'll try again in a week or two. Maybe now we should think about names."

"Do you have any suggestions?" Joe asked.

"I was thinking if he is a boy, we can name him after you."

"You want to name him 'Josip?' Are you sure?"

"How about 'Joseph?'"

"Joseph is fine with me. What if she is a girl?"

"I don't know. What do you think?"

"I like Elizabeth. It was my adoptive mother's name."

"I think that's a great name," Katie said. "It was also my grandmother's name."

"Okay, then. It's settled. That was easy."

***

"Will that be just for tonight?" asked the old man behind the counter at The Lone Wolf Motel."

"That's right. Just one night," said the man with the dark sunglasses.

"That will be seventy-five dollars," the old man said.

The man with the sunglasses handed him a credit card.

The old man entered the card number into the computer and handed him a key and a receipt. He said, "You are in room number four. Just out the door and to the left."

He took his key and went to his car to retrieve a couple of bags, a laptop, and the small computer he had taken from the Three Eagles Resort. He went inside his room, set everything down on the bed, and showered. When finished, he took clothes out of one of the bags and dressed. Since he didn't have a change of clothes with him, he stopped at a big box store and bought clothes, food, and other needed supplies.

He took a small tool kit out of one of the bags and set the computer on the bed. He turned it upside down and unscrewed the cover. He lifted it off, unscrewed the small hard drive, and removed it. He took an adaptor from the bag and plugged it into the hard drive. He then opened the laptop, turned it on, and plugged the other end of the adaptor into it.

He was by no means a computer expert, but he knew how to find a hidden file. After several minutes, he located what he was looking for and played it. He could tell it was two men talking, but hearing what they were talking about was difficult. He turned up the volume but still couldn't make it out.

He picked up the phone and dialed a number.

"Did you find it yet?" asked the man on the other end.

"I did. Parker downloaded it to one of their computers. I have the computer now. What do you want me to do with it?"

"I want you to destroy it. What about backups? Did they have back-ups for that computer?"

"I don't know. I didn't think to stop and ask while I was stealing it."

"Well, you need to get back there and find out."

"How do you suggest I do that?"

"I don't know. Isn't that what I pay you for?"

The man hung up the phone. He wished he were using a landline so he could slam the receiver.

He formatted the hard drive, filled the sink with water, and dropped it into it. Then he sat on the bed, turned the television on, and relaxed. He would return to the resort, but only when he felt like it.

Chapter 11

Katie and Joe arrived at the resort before nine the next morning. Susan was behind the front desk. "Hi, Susan," Joe said and kissed her on the cheek. "Are you working here again?"

"Hi, Dad. Yes, retirement is boring, and thanks to you, I have had so much energy lately. I told Michael I wanted to come back a couple of days a week."

"That's great, Susan, but I don't think we can afford your salary," Joe said, laughing.

Susan smiled and said, "When I was a little girl, people would sometimes ask what my father did for a living. I always told them you were a photographer, but you thought you were a comedian."

Katie laughed. "That's funny. Knowing Joe, I believe that story."

"Well, Susan," Joe said. "The apple really doesn't fall far from the tree."

When they entered the office, Michael was working at his desk. "Good morning, Pops. Good morning, Katie," he said.

"Good morning, Michael," Joe said. "This day is full of surprises. I didn't expect you to be here on a Saturday."

"It was pretty busy this week, and I got behind on some of my work. I plan on going home in an hour or so. Eric is here, too. He drove to the electronics store to buy a computer to replace the stolen one."

"That's a good half-hour drive. Why didn't he just order it and have it delivered?"

"He remembered something last night and wanted to surprise you."

"Really? What did he remember?" Joe asked.

"If I told you, it wouldn't be a surprise," Michael said.

Joe looked at Katie, who shrugged. "Okay. I guess we'll just have to wait."

Eric arrived forty-five minutes later with a computer in his hand. "I hear you have a surprise for us," Joe said.

"I sure do."

Eric opened one of the cabinets in the office and took out a portable hard drive. "Follow me," he said before leading them to the business center. He took the small computer out of the box and set it where the stolen one had been. "I was thinking yesterday that our main computers are backed up to the cloud, but these three are not," he said as he connected the computer to the cables left behind by the thief.

"If these computers aren't backed up, what's the surprise?" Katie asked.

He held up the small portable hard drive. "I decided to back these computers up before the end of the year. There's nothing important on any of them, but I thought having a backup would make it easier to restore if one crashed or was stolen, as in this case."

Joe stepped out of the room and looked around. The only person he saw was a guest sitting in one of the chairs in the lobby, reading a magazine. He returned inside and closed the door behind him. "You mean Parker's recording could be on that thing?"

"If Parker copied something onto this computer in November, it should be here."

"That's great," Joe said. "Can't you just search that thing from another computer?"

"No. It's saved as an image file, so I have to download the entire file first."

"How long will that take?"

Eric finished connecting everything and turned the computer on. "I'm not sure. Maybe an hour or two."

"Okay," Joe said. "I doubt the killer is still around, but keep this door locked whenever you're alone in here."

Katie returned to the office and worked on marketing while Joe helped Susan with the guests. Twenty minutes later, Eric joined them. "The file is downloading now," he said. "The remaining time is about forty-five minutes."

"Does this have something to do with that killing and Katie's kidnapping?" Susan asked.

"We think so. We believe there is something on that computer that could put some powerful people in prison," Joe said.

"Oh, my. So that's what this is all about and not the jewels?"

"We think the story about missing jewels might have been fabricated."

"You sure have seen more than your share of drama lately, Dad."

"Ain't that the truth?"

When the backup finished downloading, Eric alerted Joe and Katie. They all went to the business center, and Eric sat at the computer. "So, what are we looking for?" he asked.

"We are looking for an audio file," Joe said.

"Can you be more specific?" Eric asked.

"Not really. Can you search by date?" Katie asked.

"Sure. What date are we looking for?"

"November 4th," Katie said.

Eric typed in a search query, and after a few seconds, six files showed up on the screen. Five were too small to be anything significant, but the sixth was an audio file. Katie pointed at it and said, "I think that's it."

Eric double-clicked the file, and the media player opened it and started playing the recording. They could hear talking, but it was difficult to understand what they were saying. "Can you turn it up?" Joe asked.

Eric raised the volume, but that only increased the background noise. "I still can't understand what they are saying," Joe said.

"Maybe Billy can filter out the background," Katie said.

"Isn't he off on the weekends?" Joe asked.

"Yes. I forgot it's Saturday."

"I might know someone who can help," Eric said. "A friend of mine is a musician who works a lot with audio files. I'll bet he'll know what to do."

"That's great," Katie said. "Do you think he can do it right away?"

"I'll send it to him and see what he says."

Eric attached the file to an email and asked for help cleaning up the audio. He then took out his phone and texted his friend. He asked him to check his email and said it was very important. "I should know soon," Eric said.

Thirty seconds later, Eric got a reply saying, "No problem. I should have it for you in less than an hour."

***

True to his word, Eric's friend texted him back a little less than an hour later. "Your file is ready. Check your email. WTF? That's crazy shit. Who is that?"

Eric texted him back. "Thanks. It's complicated. I'll tell you when I know more."

Eric informed Joe and Katie that the file was ready. They met in the business office, and Eric played the file from his email. This time, the voices were much easier to understand. "I think we need to go to plan B," the first voice said.

"You want to take out Erikson?" asked the second voice.

"Can you think of a better solution?"

"I guess not, but killing him might backfire."

"I agree. We won't kill him. We'll kill someone else and make him take the fall for it. I know a guy who can do it for a price."

There were a few seconds of silence before the second guy said, "Okay, let's do it."

The recording ended, and Katie said, "Holy shit!"

"What is it?" Joe asked.

"Daniel Erikson is a state congressman who was running against Ford for the Democratic nomination for U.S. Senator. He was favored to beat Ford, but his wife was killed, and he was accused of her murder. I believe he is on trial for it as we speak."

"Are you certain?" Joe asked.

Katie took out her phone and looked it up. "Yes. The trial started on Monday." She continued to look at her phone and said, "The murder happened five days after Parker made this recording."

"It looks like Ford took out his main competitor, and we have the proof," Joe said.

"No, you don't," came a husky voice from the doorway. Everyone turned to look and saw a man wearing dark sunglasses, a hat, and a mask. The same man who stole the first computer and kidnapped Katie. This time, he was wearing a different hat. He pointed his gun at Eric and said, "Give me the computer and the backup drive."

"No!" came a voice from behind the man. It was loud and stern. "You've caused enough problems for these people."

The man turned and saw Jack Rosko pointing a gun at him. He pointed his gun at Jack, who said, "I suspected you were crooked, Bill, but I never thought you would stoop to murder. Put your gun down. It's over."

Bill West pulled his mask down and removed his glasses, "I guess you don't know me as well as you thought." He pulled the trigger. The bullet entered Jack's chest and sent him backward just as Jack's gun went off and hit Bill in the chest. Both men hit the ground at the same time.

"Call 911!" Katie yelled to Eric, who took his phone out of his pocket and dialed.

Joe knelt between the two men and grabbed each of their wrists. He had never connected with two people at the same time before, but he surprised himself and could feel both men. Bill West was hit in the heart and was fading fast. Joe knew he had only seconds, not enough time to save him. His life force faded quickly, and then Joe felt nothing from the man.

He let go of Bill West and concentrated on Jack Rosko's injury. The bullet narrowly missed Jack's heart, puncturing his right lung and causing him severe difficulty in breathing. Joe knew exactly how he felt. Several days earlier, Joe was shot in the back, puncturing one of his lungs. Breathing required most of his concentration, so he connected with Katie and let her be the healer.

This time, Joe was able to concentrate fully on the problem. The bullet nicked one of Jack's ribs, but fortunately, it didn't break apart. Joe instructed Jack's body to push the bullet away from the lung to an area where it wouldn't cause any problems. He then worked on healing the lung. He didn't want to heal it too much, which might draw unwanted attention, but he wanted to get Jack's breathing under control before the paramedics arrived.

Joe's eyes were closed, but he could hear Katie. She had knelt on Jack's other side and was trying to comfort him. "You'll be okay. Relax and concentrate on breathing. It will get easier. I promise."

A couple of sheriff's deputies arrived first. Eric led them out of the room to the lobby and explained what had happened. A few minutes later, the paramedics arrived. By then, Jack's breathing had normalized.

Katie and Joe left the room while the paramedics examined Jack's injury. Over a dozen people gathered, curious to see what was happening. Detective Conner entered the lobby and, after seeing Katie and Joe, pushed her way through the crowd to talk to them. "I heard on the radio you had another shooting."

"Yes," Katie said. She pointed to the business center. "Two people were shot. The guy who kidnapped me is dead. The other guy saved us. It's Jack Rosko."

"Jack Rosko saved you? You mean the shady cop who used his vacation to stalk a former criminal?"

"The very one," Joe said. "It seems he's not so bad after all. His partner was the killer. His name is Bill West."

"Interesting," Conner said. "Why did he return? I mean, he got what he wanted. Why would he want to come back?"

"He probably suspected we had a backup, and he was right. After we restored it to a new computer, he showed up and demanded the new computer and the backup drive."

"We had already sent a copy to an audio expert to have it cleaned up, so even if we gave him what he wanted, it wouldn't have mattered," Katie said. "Jack Rosko showed up while he had a gun on us. He tried to get him to surrender, but West just shot him. Jack shot back, and it seems the best man won."

"So, what happened to Jack Rosko? Will he be okay?"

"I'm sure he'll be fine," Katie said. "He was very lucky."

The paramedics wheeled Jack out of the room, and when they passed Katie and Joe, he asked them to stop. He grabbed Joe's arm and said, "I don't know what you did or how you did it, but thank you."

"I didn't do anything," Joe said.

"I heard about you Healers, but I thought you were just a legend. I never thought I would meet one."

Joe and Katie looked at each other in shock. One of the paramedics said, "We have to go," and they wheeled Jack out the door and put him in the ambulance.

"What did he mean by 'Healers?'" Connor asked.

"Your guess is as good as mine," Joe said.

"I heard people sometimes get delusional after being shot," Katie added.

"That's a new one on me," Connor said. "I suppose it's possible, though."

"You have your killer and your kidnapper. What will you do now?" Joe asked.

"I think we can wrap this case up, but I'd like to hear that recording you were talking about."

"It's on the computer in there," Katie said. "I'd prefer to wait until the body is removed."

"You said you sent it to an audio expert. Did you get it back?"

"Yes. Eric knew a guy who helped get rid of the background noise," Katie said.

"Did he email it back to you? Do you have it on your phone?"

"No, but I think Eric can get it. I doubt you will need it, though. It would be more relevant to the Milwaukee Police Department."

"Maybe so, but I still want to hear it."

Katie saw Eric on the other side of the crowd and waved him over.

He walked over and asked, "Do you need something, Katie?"

"Can you get the email your friend sent you on your phone?"

"I think so," Eric said and took out his phone. He opened his email app and, after a few seconds, said, "Here it is."

He handed the phone to Katie, who played the file. They all listened, and when it was over, Connor said, "That's messed up. I can see why someone would kill to keep that hidden." Connor had given Katie a business card after the first murder, but handed her another and said, "Please email that file to me."

Katie forwarded her the email with the attached file and sent another copy to her own email before handing the phone back to Eric. She asked the detective, "Do you have everything you need now?"

"I think so. As soon as the coroner's office picks up the body, we will be out of your hair. I'm sorry you have another mess to clean up."

"Thanks. I don't know how we will spin this one. People will be afraid to come here now."

"Your Captain friend says you two are good investigators. Maybe if you help bring those men to justice, it will be good publicity for this place."

"I think we've done enough investigating," Joe said. "We'll just turn this recording over to the police, and they can handle Ford."

"I don't think it will be that easy," Katie said.

"Why not?" Joe asked.

"Well, I was about to mention something, but then all this craziness happened, and I never got the chance."

"Okay. What were you going to mention?"

"Mayor Ford was not one of the voices on that recording."

"I see you two have your work cut out for you," Connor said. "I need to get back to work. I wish you the best of luck."

Chapter 12

It was well after lunchtime when Connor and the deputies finished their work and left the resort. Katie and Joe ordered a couple of sandwiches from the restaurant and ate them on the road as they headed to the hospital to see Jack Rosko.

"Does it worry you that Jack Rosko knows what you are?" Katie asked.

"A little, but it is only speculation on his part. Plus, he seemed pretty appreciative. I doubt he would cause problems for me."

"I hope you're right."

When they reached the hospital, a friendly volunteer directed them to Jack's room. They found him alone. The door was open, but Katie knocked and asked, "Is it okay if we come in?"

"Of course," Jack said. "It's good to see you two again. Have a seat."

Chairs were positioned on either side of the bed. Joe moved one to the other side and sat next to Katie. "We came to see how you are doing," Katie said.

"I'm doing great, thanks to Joe. The doctors can't understand how the bullet missed all my vital organs. They think it's a miracle."

"What did you tell them?" Joe asked.

"I told them God must be looking out for me. I couldn't tell them the truth. They would have thought I was crazy."

"Maybe God is looking out for you," Joe said.

"Maybe he is. Maybe he put you in my path."

Joe realized he wasn't going to change Jack's mind, so he decided he had no choice but to trust him. "What do you know about the Healers?"

"Just what I learned from my grandmother. My grandparents came to America from the old country, Hungary. The story I heard was that my grandmother's grandfather had developed an infection in his eyes that left him almost totally blind. Nobody locally could help him, and they couldn't afford to take him to a specialist. They heard that there was a healer not far over the Croatian border, so my great-great-grandmother borrowed a horse and wagon and traveled to where the healer was rumored to live. It took a couple of days, but they found the Healer, who cured my great-great-grandfather of his blindness through a simple touch. Not only that, he charged them only what they could afford to pay and put them up for the night before they headed home."

"Did you believe that story when your grandmother told it to you?" Joe asked.

"I was pretty young at the time, so yeah. I believed it. As I got older, I had doubts. I thought maybe he used some herbs or something like that. Since I heard the story second-hand, it could have been altered or exaggerated. Now I know it was true."

"Can I trust you to keep this under your hat?" Joe asked.

"Of course. Who would believe me anyway?"

"The Healer you refer to was an ancestor of mine."

"That makes sense. You must be a family of do-gooders."

"I never knew my family. I was an orphan. I only recently learned the history of my birth family."

"Well, now you know more," Jack said.

"There's another reason we came here," Katie said. "Bobby Parker recorded a conversation between two men at Ford's house the day he broke in. He copied it to one of our computers. It is the reason he came back to the resort. His phone was confiscated, and the recording never came to light."

"So that's what this was all about?" Jack asked.

"Yes. We believe the story about missing jewels was fabricated."

"Why would they lie about missing jewels?"

"We are assuming it was a lie, but we don't yet know the motivation for lying," Katie said. "Ford never received a payment from his insurance company. But it is clear that Bobby's motivation for coming here was to retrieve the recording. His wife said he wanted to make things right."

Jack was silent for a few seconds and asked, "So if this was about the recording, what was on it that was so damn important? Do you have this recording with you?" Jack asked.

"We do," Katie said. She took out her phone, found the file, and started playing it.

Jack listened to it and said, "It seems I was a fool. I thought his punishment was too lenient. I wanted to catch him with the jewels."

"That's understandable," Joe said. "They needed to find Parker fast after the break-in, so they had to make him look like a worse criminal than he really was.

Now that I think about it, that could have been their motivation to lie about the jewels."

"I can't believe Bill was involved in something so cold-blooded. It was he and I who were first on the scene after Erickson's wife was murdered. Bill found the murder weapon in the trash can outside. It didn't occur to me then that it was too easy."

"What exactly happened?" Joe asked. "How did you end up there first?"

"It was evening. Bill had a craving for a hamburger, so we stopped at a burger joint just down the street from Erikson's house. We got a call that someone had heard gunshots from that location. Since we were already close, we got there before anyone else."

"It seems your partner knew what was about to happen and wanted to be there before anyone else," Joe said.

"Yes. That seems obvious now."

"So, now we have another killer out there to find," Katie said. "Was Erikson at the house when you arrived?"

"Yes. He had some crazy story about someone throwing rocks at his house. He said he went outside to confront them. That's when he heard two gunshots from inside his house. He ran back into his house and found his wife dead on the living room floor. At the time, I thought it was a pretty lame excuse, but now I feel like I have to rethink how I look at everything. I have been so wrong about too many people."

"Did you recognize either of the voices on the audio?" Katie asked. "I didn't recognize Ford's voice."

"Sorry, I'm afraid neither sounds familiar to me."

"Can you think of any reason anyone would go into Ford's house while he was away?" Joe asked.

"Well, the house technically belongs to Ford's father, so maybe it was him. The scuttlebutt is that Ford is under the thumb of his father. He doesn't take a shit without his approval. At least, that's what I heard."

"Even if the house is in his name, it seems rude to just show up there while Ford and his wife are away," Katie said.

"I doubt if guys like that care about manners. Ford's house is much closer to downtown than his father's house. If his father were to arrange a meeting with someone, that house would be a good choice."

"So one of the guys is probably Ford's father. Who do you think the other guy is?" Katie asked.

"I don't know," Jack said. "It would be someone who has a vested interest in Ford winning the Senator's election, or someone Ford's father is paying a lot of money to help get his son into the senate. I'm sure having a United States senator in your pocket must be worth a fortune."

"It looks like we have our work cut out for us," Katie said.

"Thank you so much for your time," Joe said.

"If you're not in a hurry, can you finish what you started? Can you fix the damage to my lung?"

"I hesitate to do anything that can't be explained. It would draw too much attention to me."

"I wouldn't worry about that. These doctors think that the bullet missed all my vital organs."

Joe looked at Katie, who nodded. "Okay. We don't have time to make you perfect, but I can repair most of the damage I didn't have a chance to fix earlier. Your body can probably take care of the rest."

"Okay. That's all I can ask for."

Joe held Jack's hand and connected with him. He didn't allow Jack to feel what he was feeling. He didn't think Jack would betray him, but he also figured the less he knew, the better. Joe continued the repairs that he started earlier. He only worked on the lung and the areas around it. He didn't try to fix the scars left by the bullet and the surgeons. That would have been too obvious. After about thirty minutes, Joe let go and said, "If you don't start smoking, that lung should last you a good long while. I think Katie and I should get back to the resort now. I hope the next time I see you, it will be for a real vacation."

"I think now is a good time. My wife is on her way here. I'll suggest to her that we spend a couple of days at the resort after the hospital releases me. I think the department can give me a little more time off, considering my own partner shot me."

"That's a wonderful idea," Katie said. "I would like to meet your wife and tell her what you did for us."

"I look forward to meeting your wife as well," Joe said.

***

As they left the hospital and walked to the car, Katie said, "Since we came this far, let's stay and have dinner in town."

"That's fine with me. What do you feel like eating?"

"I don't know. Let's drive until we see something interesting."

After getting in the car and putting their seatbelts on, Joe said, "If you leave the parking lot and turn left, we will be heading toward downtown. We should find something interesting that way."

Katie turned left, and after a few minutes, they passed a Mexican restaurant. Joe watched it go by and said, "I take it you don't want Mexican."

"No. I'm not in the mood for it today."

Katie drove past an Italian restaurant, a seafood restaurant, and a classic fifties diner. "Are you not hungry?" Joe asked.

Katie saw something that looked appealing and parked the car. They were in front of a small building that served hot dogs. It was take-out only, but they had picnic tables set up outside.

"Hotdogs?" Joe asked. "I figured you might want something fancy."

"You should know me by now, Joe. I may act like a prima donna sometimes, but deep down, I also enjoy the simple things. When I was young, around ten or twelve years old, my dad had a motorcycle and sometimes took me for a ride around town. We always ended up at this little hot dog stand before he took me home. It was very similar to this one. I know it's a little thing, but those are fond memories."

"It's not a little thing," Joe said. "It's how your father showed you love, which is never a little thing."

Katie leaned over and kissed Joe. "I probably shouldn't tell you this because I don't want it to go to your head, but I feel the same way when you cook for me. Now, let's go have a hot dog."

They got out of the car and went to the order window. The smell drifting through the air was just how Katie remembered it. They ordered a couple of hot dogs with fries and sat at a picnic table when the food was ready. "These are just like the hot dogs I remember with my dad," Katie said.

"I'm glad you like them. If you want, I can make these for you at home."

"Can you take me for a ride on your motorcycle first?"

"How about a ride on an ATV?"

"Oh, you told me you would take me to see the eaglets. When are you going to do that?"

"Let's get up early tomorrow. We can go out for an hour before work."

"Okay, but that means we can't stay up half the night having sex."

"If you say so. We'll have to limit ourselves to two hours."

Katie looked at her watch and said, "Okay. We need to go home as soon as we finish eating."

Chapter 13

The following morning, Katie and Joe woke up to an alarm that Katie had set on her phone. She pressed the snooze button and asked, "Can we forget about the eagles this morning and go back to bed?"

"No. You will regret it if you miss it. Besides, you were the one who wanted to stay up past midnight making love."

"I didn't hear any complaints from you," Katie said.

"Let's get up. I'll make you a strong cup of coffee."

"Okay. Wake me when the coffee's ready."

Joe got up and started brewing a pot of coffee. He didn't bother putting on any clothes. When the coffee started brewing, he got back into bed with Katie and rolled on top of her. He kissed her, and Katie said, "I'm definitely up now, and so are you, I see. I like your alarm clock so much better than mine."

They arrived at the resort just before seven. Joe got his camera and led Katie to the garage, where they stored the ATVs. He pointed to a dark red one and said, "You can take that one. It's made for beginners."

"Can't I just ride with you, Joe?"

"You can, but I think you will enjoy having your own."

"Are you sure it's safe?"

"Everything is a risk, Katie. You said it yourself."

"I know, but I mean, how risky is it?"

"If you pay attention to what I tell you, you'll be fine."

"Oh, I hear some bossiness coming out of your mouth. I think I like it."

Joe explained to Katie how to operate the ATV and some safety precautions. They then left the garage and headed down the trail and up the mountain. Katie followed Joe, and they rode to the top before stopping. They walked to the clearing and looked out at the resort.

Katie took a deep breath. The smell of the trees permeated the air, and combined with the view, it made for a perfect moment in time. "The last time I saw this view was when you brought me here on a snowmobile after we met," Katie said.

"Yes. It is beautiful when there is snow on the ground, but spring has its advantages."

Joe took Katie's hand and led her through the trees until they came upon another clearing. Katie saw both eagles perched on their nest, watching over the two eaglets inside. Her eyes widened. "This is amazing," she said. "We are so close."

Joe took his camera off his shoulder and started snapping pictures. The morning sun illuminated the birds perfectly. He put his camera back over his shoulder and asked, "Do you want to go, or should we stay a little longer?"

"Let's stay five more minutes. I want to get a picture to send to my parents." She took out her phone and said, "Stand next to me."

Joe stood next to Katie, who carefully aligned herself, Joe, and the eagles in the frame before snapping the picture. She then texted it to her mother.

After they returned to the resort and put the ATVs away, Katie said, "That was a lot of fun. We should do that again sometime."

"Of course. The eaglets should be there for several more weeks."

They walked to the front desk, where a couple of weekend employees were working. They said hello, and Joe joined Katie in the office since he was not needed at the front desk. He rolled Michael's chair next to Katie and sat down. "I assume you will want to look into those voices on the recording," he said.

"You read my mind. I'm looking to see what Ford's father's name is."

Katie first looked up Timothy Ford and found a page about him. She scanned the page, looking for his parents' names. "Here it is," she said. "His mother, Eva, died in 2013. His father, Gideon Ford, retired a year later in 2014."

"Gideon? I bet he never got teased in school."

"It's not a bad name. I wouldn't have teased him."

"Of course, you wouldn't have because you are not mean like that, but some kids can be cruel."

Katie looked at Joe and asked, "Were you teased in school?"

"Me? No. I was a tough kid. Other kids pretty much left me alone. I did have a friend named Jimmy who was picked on for his red hair and freckles."

"Did you stand up for him?"

"Of course I did, but the teasing was always just teasing. It never turned violent, although other kids in school weren't so lucky."

"Did you ever tease anyone when you were a kid?"

"Maybe a little when I was very young, but once I learned that I was different, I didn't want to cause problems for other kids who were also different."

"I doubt if other kids were as different as you," Katie said.

"You never know," Joe said. "Maybe one of my classmates was the inspiration for Clark Kent?"

"Clark Kent is not a real person."

"How do you know? What if you drew a comic book and called it 'The Last Healer?' You would change my name, and nobody would ever think it was true."

Katie shook her head. "You have quite an imagination. Can we get back to Gideon Ford now?"

"Of course. Can you find a recording of him speaking?"

"I'm looking now," Katie said.

"Maybe we can look up his phone number and call him."

"No. We're not going to call him. This isn't the eighties. We have this thing called the internet now."

"Very funny."

"I found something," Katie said. "It's a Ford Jewelry commercial from 2010. Gideon Ford is speaking."

"You mean someone went through the trouble of saving an old commercial to the internet?"

"You would be amazed at what you can find online."

Katie hit play on the old commercial, and they listened closely. When it was over, Joe asked, "Can you play the other recording?"

Katie found the audio file and hit play. They listened to it, and Joe said, "I think he is the second voice. Let's hear the commercial again."

Katie played the commercial again, and they both agreed that the second voice was Gideon Ford. "Now we need to figure out who the first guy is," Katie said.

"Do you have any ideas?" Joe asked.

"I don't have a clue."

"I know who would know."

Katie looked surprised. "You do? Who?"

"Timothy Ford."

"Oh, yes. I'm sure the man who benefited from a woman's murder will help us ruin his political career and possibly send him to jail."

"Sometimes you have to shake the tree," Joe said.

Katie was silent for several seconds and finally said, "You're right. Let's shake Ford's tree and see what falls out."

"Okay, I'm up for that, but remember, these people are killers. We need to give that recording to someone and make it clear there are copies out there."

"That's a good idea," Katie said, typing an email to Bob Martin. She attached the recording to the email and explained what it was and where they got the recording. She also sent a copy of the email to Gabe."

Joe waited until Katie finished sending the emails and said, "Bob Martin might be able to help get us an appointment with the mayor."

"You're right. He does have a lot more influence than I do."

Katie took out her phone and dialed Bob Martin's cell phone number. "Hello, Katie," Bob said. "What's up?"

"Hi, Bob. Sorry to bother you on the weekend, but it's important."

"It's fine. Is everything okay?"

"I sent an audio file to your email. It's evidence that Mayor Ford's father and another man conspired to murder Daniel Erikson's wife to help Ford get nominated."

"Wow! You've been busy. Is this related to the murder at your resort?"

"Yes. Bobby Parker made the recording when he broke into Mayor Ford's house. He hid it on a computer at the resort and returned to retrieve it when he got out of jail. There were never any jewels stolen from Ford's house. That was a lie."

"It sounds like you decided to investigate this case after all."

"Yes, so I need you to extend my employment for a few more days."

"I never ended it. I knew you would change your mind."

"We also need your help, which is why we're calling. We want you to try to get us an appointment to see the mayor tomorrow."

"Oh, so you want to enter the lions' den, huh?"

"I think it's our best option right now."

"Okay. I'll call first thing tomorrow morning and see what I can do. Just be careful."

"Don't worry. This won't be like last time."

After Katie hung up, she called Michael and told him they were returning to Milwaukee for a couple of days. They then went home and packed.

Once they were on the road, Katie asked, "Do you think what we are doing is stupid?"

"Yes, but I've realized that we each have a purpose in life, and suppressing that purpose never turns out well."

Katie held Joe's hand and said, "You are a smart man, Josip Novak."

"Probably more wise than smart."

"What's the difference?"

"Knowledge is learned, wisdom is earned."

Katie's phone rang before she could respond. It was Gabe. She answered the call and said, "Hi, Gabe."

"Hi, Katie. That's an unbelievable recording you sent me. How did you get it?"

"It's a long story. In a nutshell, Parker recorded it the day he broke into Ford's house. He copied it to one of the resort's computers the day he was arrested. The jewel heist was a lie. The recording is what Parker returned to the resort to retrieve. Unfortunately, he was killed before he could get it. We'll explain everything when we see you. We are heading back to Milwaukee now."

"Where will you stay? Maybe we can meet for dinner."

Katie looked at Joe, who shrugged. "We'll stay at the same hotel we were at last week," she said.

"Okay. We'll see you tonight."

***

When Katie and Joe arrived at the hotel and checked in, they were starving. They had skipped breakfast but decided it would be better to wait until they arrived in Milwaukee rather than stop and get fast food. They went to their room first to drop off their luggage, but were soon in the throes of passion. They made love and then lay together on the bed.

"The Beatles must have written 'All you need is love' after they ate lunch," Katie joked. "I'm starving."

"Man cannot live on sex alone," Joe replied with a grin. "It's in the Bible."

Katie looked at Joe, smiled, and shook her head. "I just don't know about you sometimes."

Joe laughed and said, "Okay. Let's get up and have lunch."

They headed to the hotel's restaurant, where they were seated immediately. After they ordered, Joe said, "Milwaukee is starting to feel like a second home."

"Maybe I'll make a city boy out of you yet."

"Not likely. I grew up in a city. I much prefer the simple life."

"Don't worry. I wouldn't take you away from what you love. Besides, I love where we live, too."

"Really? You don't regret leaving Milwaukee?"

"No. I thought I would, but I don't. I grew up in a small town and felt restless as a teenager. I wanted to be where the action was, but now that I'm older, I no longer feel that way. Perhaps I just needed to get it out of my system."

"I think that's common among teenagers from every generation."

Their server came with their food just as Katie's phone rang. She saw it was Gabe calling. She let it ring and answered it after the server left. She put the call on speaker so Joe could hear. "Hi, Gabe."

"Hi, Katie. Hi Joe. Carmen is looking forward to seeing you two tonight. She thinks you guys are really cool for young people."

Katie laughed. "So I assume you haven't told her."

"I promised to keep your secret, and I'm a man of my word. I won't lie to my wife, but what she doesn't know won't hurt her."

"Thanks, Gabe," Joe said. "Where do you two want to go for dinner tonight?"

"How do you guys feel about Japanese food?"

Katie looked at Joe, who nodded. "That sounds great," she said. "I haven't had Japanese food in ages."

"Good. The place is just a couple of blocks from your hotel, going toward Veterans' Park."

"I know the place, Gabe," Katie said. "When would you like to meet?"

"We assumed you would be okay with it, so we took the liberty of making a reservation for six o'clock. I hope that's not too early for you. We both have to work tomorrow and don't want to be out too late."

"Six is perfect. We'll meet you there," Katie said.

When she hung up, Katie looked at her watch and then at her plate. "I think we should skip dessert," she said.

"We usually do," Joe said.

When they finished eating lunch, they went back to their room. Katie took out her laptop and sat on the bed with it.

"What are you doing?" Joe asked.

"Marketing. I thought since we are at a standstill on this case, I could use this time to get some of my marketing work done."

"I like your dedication."

"I actually enjoy my new job. I see it as a challenge. Right now, I still have a lot of learning to do, but I think I can really make a difference."

"You are a smart woman, Katie. I know you will be great at this job."

Joe took a photography magazine from the suitcase. He sat next to Katie and started reading. When he finished, he put the magazine on the nightstand. Katie stopped what she was doing and asked, "Did you learn anything interesting?"

"Film cameras are becoming popular again."

"So are vinyl records," Katie said. "I think people like to be nostalgic."

"Sometimes the old ways are better."

"I get it. Except for your camera, you have almost nothing modern. If we ever had an extended power outage, you would barely notice. I admire that about you. I would be a basket case without my phone."

"I think you are tougher than you think you are."

"I don't know. I hope we never have to find out." Katie said as she closed her laptop. "I think we still have time to finish our shopping."

"What shopping?" Joe asked.

"Don't tell me you forgot. The last time we were here, we did some shopping and decided to wait until we returned from our walk to buy what we found."

"I remember," Joe said.

"And then you got yourself shot, so that didn't happen."

"Are you implying that was my fault?"

"No. I'm just saying, now is a great time to finish what we started. Plus, it's a beautiful day for a walk."

"Okay, my love. Let's finish our shopping."

Katie took Joe's hand, and they left the hotel. It was indeed a beautiful day. The sun was shining, and the temperature was a perfect seventy degrees. The last time they were in Milwaukee, they needed a jacket most of the time, but now they could leave their jackets in their room.

They crossed the street and walked to the shopping district. Katie remembered which stores had the items she wanted, and one by one, the bags Joe had to carry became heavier. Eventually, they arrived at the camera store, where Joe wanted to purchase a 360-degree camera. The camera was small and lightweight, but after the saleswoman rang him up and put his camera in a bag, Joe handed the bag to Katie. "It's only fair," he said.

When they returned to their room, Katie said, "We still have almost two hours. What do you want to do?"

Joe put his arms around Katie, kissed her, and said, "Do you really need to ask?"

***

Katie and Joe decided walking to the restaurant would be easier than driving, so Katie wore her casual walking shoes. Joe wore his sneakers, as usual. He packed dress shoes, but he hated wearing them. His wide feet made finding dress shoes that didn't pinch his toes difficult.

The Japanese restaurant was in the middle of the shopping district, sandwiched between a women's clothing store and a music store.

"Did you ever learn to play a musical instrument?" Katie asked.

"My mother sent me to take piano lessons when I was fifteen. She thought it would be good for me to try different things."

"How good did you get?"

"Well, with much practice, I was able to make it all the way up to terrible, which was good because I was horrible when I started."

Katie laughed and said, "That's okay. The radio was the only musical instrument I ever learned how to play."

"I bet you were the best radio player on your block," Joe said.

Katie laughed. "I don't know. My friend Jenna was really good at finding the right station."

They went inside the restaurant and saw Gabe and Carmen waiting for them. After greeting each other, the hostess picked up some menus and led them to a table surrounding a large grill. Three people sat at the far end of the table: a man, a woman, and a young boy. Joe sat near the family, leaving an empty seat between them. Katie sat on Joe's left while Carmen and Gabe took the last two chairs.

Carmen wore a tight black dress, while Gabe was dressed semi-casually, wearing a polo shirt and tan slacks. In contrast, Katie and Joe were both dressed casually. Katie wore a low-cut sweater and blue jeans. Joe also wore blue jeans, but with a plain blue T-shirt.

"You look beautiful," Katie said to Carmen. "I wish I knew we needed to dress up."

"You didn't need to dress up. Besides, you look gorgeous the way you are."

"We're both looking forward to hearing about what happened at the resort and how you ended up here," Gabe said.

Joe looked at Katie and said, "Why don't you tell them, Honey?"

A man interrupted them and took everyone's drink order. When he left, Katie told them the entire story, including her kidnapping and Bill West's death. She also explained everything about the recording she sent Gabe. While she was telling the story, the man arrived with the drinks. He took everyone's food order and left again.

Katie continued with the story. When she finished, the guy sitting at the end of their table said, "Wow! I'm sorry to eavesdrop, but that was an incredible story."

"Watch Channel 23 News," Katie said. "Hopefully, we'll have something to report in a day or two."

"Are you a reporter?" The woman asked.

"I am today," Katie said.

"That is so cool," the woman said. "We never met anyone famous before."

"I'm not exactly famous," Katie said.

"You're close enough. Do you mind if we get a picture with you?"

Katie looked at Joe, who nodded. "Okay," she said.

The family stood behind Katie and Joe while the man tried to get everyone in the frame, including himself. Gabe stood up and said, "Let me do that."

The man handed his phone to Gabe, who took a photo and then handed the phone back. "Thank you so much," he said.

When they all returned to their seats, the chef arrived. He greeted everyone and started cooking their meals. During the meal, they mainly talked about personal matters. The investigation seemed unimportant. After they finished eating and paid their checks, they said their goodbyes. Gabe offered to drive them back to the hotel, but Katie and Joe thought walking off the big meal they had just eaten would be good.

The temperature had dropped while they were inside the restaurant, and it was a bit cold outside. They now regretted that they didn't bring their jackets. Joe put his arm around Katie to help keep her warm as they walked.

Most of the stores they walked by were closed. They saw a young man sitting on the ground, leaning against a lamppost. He appeared to be sleeping.

"He doesn't look homeless," Joe said. "There might be something wrong with him."

"Maybe he's drunk," Katie said.

Joe knelt beside him and held his wrist. A passerby would think he was checking for a pulse, but Joe was checking for much more than that. "He's on some kind of drug," Joe said.

"What kind of drug?" Katie asked.

"I have no idea. I'm not familiar with drugs."

"No. Of course, you wouldn't be. Can you do anything for him?"

"He'll be fine after he sleeps it off, but I think I can help him after he wakes up."

After a few minutes, Joe stood up, took Katie's hand, and they continued walking.

"What did you do?" Katie asked.

"I read years ago that chronic drug use can suppress the body's ability to produce certain feel-good hormones. That makes it almost impossible for a drug user to feel good without the drug. I forced his body to give him a good dose of those hormones. Hopefully, when he wakes up, he will feel good enough not to need the drug. With luck, his body will remember how to feel good again."

Katie squeezed Joe's hand and said, "You are the only thing I need to feel good."

Chapter 14

Katie and Joe got ready early the following morning. They didn't know when they would be able to get in to see Mayor Ford and wanted to make sure they were prepared to go at a moment's notice. They ate breakfast at the hotel restaurant. While they were eating, Katie's phone rang. She looked at the screen and saw it was Bob Martin. "Good morning, Bob."

"Good morning, Katie. I have an appointment for you to see Mayor Ford, but he can only give you a few minutes at ten-thirty."

Katie looked at her watch. It was nine-fifteen. "Okay. We'll be there. Thanks so much, Bob."

"I hope you get the answers you're looking for. Be careful, though. You could be poking a tiger."

"Maybe, but that tiger will be in a cage called City Hall."

They arrived at City Hall a few minutes early and went to the mayor's office on the second floor. After checking in, they waited until the receptionist led them into the mayor's office, five minutes past their scheduled time. Mayor Ford stood up from his desk, shook their hands, and invited them to sit down.

He was a relatively handsome man. In his early fifties, at six feet tall, he was Joe's height, with dark hair greying at the temples. When he sat down, he asked, "What can I do for you?"

"You're not going to like what we have to say," Joe said, "but we need you to be honest with us."

Katie looked at Joe and back at Mayor Ford. "He's right," she said as she took out her phone and found the audio recording. "We need you to listen to something. Robert Parker, the man who broke into your home last year, recorded this on the day of the break-in. Someone murdered him the other day."

"Yes. I heard about his murder. I feel bad for his family, but sometimes karma bites you in the ass."

"It wasn't karma that killed him," Katie said as she hit play on the recording.

Ford listened to the recording. When it finished, he said, "That can't be real. Where did you get it?"

"We run the resort where Parker was arrested," Joe said. "He copied that recording onto one of our computers. Two people were killed, and my wife was kidnapped because of that recording, so don't tell us it's not real."

Ford put his hands on his head and leaned back in his chair to think.

"You know who's on the tape, don't you?" Katie asked. "One voice is your father. Who is the other man?"

Ford sighed and said, "That's Ethan O'Brian. He's my campaign manager."

"Were you aware of what they were planning?" Joe asked.

Ford shook his head. "No. Absolutely not. If this is true, I'm sick about it."

"I bet you are," Joe said. "You're on track to be the next senator because of what they did."

"I was on track until you showed up. Now my days of being mayor are over."

"You could claim it's a fake. The way politics are now, nobody gets punished for bad behavior anymore," Katie said.

"That is exactly what O'Brian will do if you try to report it. He has spent his life as a political fixer. He can turn any negative into a positive. You won't know what hit you."

"Maybe," Katie said. "We'll see."

Katie and Joe stood up to leave. When they reached the door, Ford said, "Wait. Have a seat."

They returned and sat down. Ford said, "I have lived in my father's shadow my entire life. I can't remember a time when I haven't been a disappointment to him. He pushed me into taking over his company. Then he pushed me into running for mayor. Now, he wants me to be a senator. It's never been about what I wanted."

"What do you want?" Katie asked.

"Honestly, I enjoy running the jewelry business, but I hate politics. I spend all day, every day, trying to make everyone happy, but it's impossible. I secretly hoped I would lose to Erikson. When he got hauled off to jail, I got knots in my stomach."

"So, will you help us?" Katie asked.

"I'll do what I can. I'm not sure what that could be."

"You can start by telling us why your father was at your house that day," Joe said.

"His house is a hundred years old. The entire home needed to be rewired. He stayed with me for a couple of weeks while the work was being done."

"What about the jewels?" Joe asked. "You claimed Parker stole two hundred thousand dollars' worth of jewels, but we have two people who are convinced Parker stole nothing from your home. Plus, you never filed an insurance claim. Why would you lie about that?"

"I never made any such claim," Ford said. "My father said they were stolen. He didn't trust the workers at his house, so he brought many of his valuables to my house while he was there. If Parker didn't steal any jewels, it's news to me."

"I think I know how you can help us," Joe said. "Can you get us an appointment to see Ethan O'Brian?"

"I think so, but unless you can get him to confess on camera, it's not likely to do you any good."

"I have an idea about that," Joe said.

Ford picked up his phone and dialed a number. When it was answered, he said, "Hi Ethan. Listen, I have a couple of reporters here from Channel 23 News. They would like to do a story on me and would appreciate a few comments from you. Can I send them over to see you?"

After a few seconds, Ford lowered the phone and said, "He can see you at four o'clock. Does that work for you?"

Katie and Joe looked at each other. They both nodded, and Katie said, "That will be fine."

When he hung up the phone, Ford said, "I want to do the right thing, but this will not only kill my political career, it might also hurt my business. I only ask that you make it clear to your viewers that I helped you."

Katie nodded and said, "That's reasonable."

When they left the mayor's office, Joe said, "You should ask Billy to check if Ford's father filed an insurance claim. I think I trust him, but it couldn't hurt to check out his story."

"Good idea," Katie said. She took out her phone and typed an email to Billy.

When they reached Katie's car and got in, Katie asked, "What is your idea? How are we going to get O'Brian to confess?"

"That drug addict last night gave me an idea, but I need your help to see if it will work."

105

"How can I help?"

"Take us back to the hotel, and I'll show you.

***

When they returned to the hotel, they sat together on the sofa and held hands while Joe connected to Katie. When it was over, Katie couldn't control her passion. She climbed on top of Joe and kissed him while unbuttoning his shirt. They didn't bother moving to the bed. They made love on the sofa. Afterward, they held each other for a long while before Katie said, "That was incredible. I don't mean just the sex. I mean everything. Now, promise you will never do that to me again."

"I promise," Joe said.

After getting dressed, they had lunch at the hotel's restaurant and headed to the television station. With time to kill, Katie thought visiting her old colleagues would be nice.

They entered the newsroom and found Ashley working at her desk. When she saw them, she stood and hugged them both. "I heard you were back in town. When you two got married, I thought I would see you a few times a year. Now, I can't get rid of you."

Everyone laughed, and Katie said, "I expect we will wrap things up here soon, so you may not see us for a while. Of course, you can always come and spend the weekend at the resort."

"I want to do that. Maybe we'll come up for the Fourth of July."

"That would be great," Katie said.

"It sounds like you already have this case figured out. Do you know who killed that man at your resort?"

"Yes. Unfortunately, he is dead, but we know who hired him. That will be a little harder to prove."

"Wow! You guys are amazing. You should have been cops."

"No thanks. We have enough problems. We're trying to be normal, but the universe won't let that happen," Katie said.

Joe coughed, and Katie looked at him suspiciously. "I've never heard you cough before. Are you trying to say I'm not trying to be normal?"

Joe smiled and said, "You trying to be normal is like an eagle trying not to fly."

Katie slapped Joe's arm playfully and said, "That's not true. Okay, maybe it's a little true, but who is normal, anyway?"

"Certainly not us," Joe said.

Ashley laughed. "You two crack me up. I hate to leave you, but I have to get my files over to editing."

They said their goodbyes and went to see Billy. He informed them that the elder Ford did indeed file an insurance claim for stolen diamonds.

They left Billy and went to see Bob Martin. "Did you learn anything useful at the mayor's office?" he asked.

"We learned the second man on the recording is Ethan O'Brian, Ford's campaign manager," Katie said.

"He told you that willingly?"

"He wasn't happy to hear the recording of his father and O'Brian, but he seemed sincere in his ignorance. He also seemed like he wanted to make it right. He said his father, not him, claimed the jewels were missing. Billy confirmed that Ford's father made an insurance claim."

"What are you going to do now? I've heard a lot about Ethan O'Brian. He made a living by making problems go away. Snaring him might be next to impossible."

"We have a plan," Joe said. "We have a meeting with him at four."

"Are you sure you want to do that? Going to the mayor's office is one thing. It's a public place. Going to O'Brian's office could be like two turkeys going to a Thanksgiving dinner."

"We appreciate your concern, Bob, but I feel confident for the first time in a long time. We're going to get that son of a bitch," Katie said.

"Okay. Good luck, and as always, be careful."

Chapter 15

After leaving the television station, they headed to the address Timothy Ford had given them. It was Ford's campaign headquarters, located in an old, four-story brick building near the southern end of downtown. The first floor was commercial and housed several offices. Ford's campaign office occupied the southeast corner. The top three floors were apartments.

Joe opened the door for Katie, and they stepped inside. They saw about a dozen people sitting at desks, most of them talking on the phone. To their left was a middle-aged woman seated behind a desk beneath a poster that read, "Timothy Ford for U.S. Senate." The smell of stale smoke clung to her clothes.

"Can I help you?" the woman asked before breaking into a fit of coughing.

"Yes. We have a meeting with Mr. O'Brian," Katie said.

"What are your names?"

"I'm Katie Novak, and this is my husband, Joe."

"Just a moment," the woman said as she picked up the phone and dialed a number. "Katie and Joe Novak are here to see you."

She hung up and said, "He's ready for you. Go left, and his office is the first door on the left.

They followed the woman's directions. When they turned the corner, Katie whispered, "I don't understand why people willingly do that to themselves."

"Some habits die hard."

"And take the people with them."

"It's a shame, but additions have ruined so many lives," Joe said.

When they reached the office, Katie knocked on the door and opened it. "Hi, Mr. O'Brian. I'm Katie Novak, and this is my husband, Joe. May we come in?"

"Of course," he said, standing up from his desk. He wasn't as powerful-looking as Joe expected. He looked more like an accountant, a little shorter than average, with thinning dark hair and wire-rim glasses. He shook Katie's hand as Joe closed the door behind him.

O'Brian reached over and shook Joe's hand. Joe immediately connected to him and focused on his pituitary gland. He continued to shake O'Brian's hand while he instructed the gland to release as many endorphins as possible. After a few seconds, O'Brian was starting to feel good, so Joe let go and put his hand on the back of his neck. "I would like to get a picture with you if that's okay," Joe said while continuing to force his endorphin levels higher while adding other feel-good hormones to his system, like dopamine, serotonin, and oxytocin. He didn't know the names of each hormone, but knew what they did. He looked at Katie. "Can you take our picture, Honey?"

They had practiced what they would do, so Katie took out her phone, set it to video mode, and started recording.

"Ford's father told us what you did to Erickson's wife. Killing her was genius. Did you think of that?" Joe asked casually.

"Yep," O'Brian said, laughing. "That's why I make the big bucks."

"Pinning it on Erikson was perfect. How did you pull it off?"

"O'Brian laughed again. "It helps to have a couple of cops on your payroll."

"Of course it does. I'd love to meet them and shake their hands. What are their names?"

"O'Brian was laughing almost uncontrollably. He put a finger to his lips. "Shhhh. It's a secret. I can't tell you."

"You can tell us," Joe said. "We won't tell anyone."

"Nope," he said, laughing. "I know how to keep a secret."

"It's okay. I can keep a secret, too," Joe said. "You can tell me."

"Nope, nope, nope," O'Brian said, now laughing uncontrollably.

Katie looked at Joe and shook her head. She turned off her camera and said, "I think we've taken enough of your time, Mr. O'Brian."

"It was fun meeting you," O'Brian finally said after forcing himself to stop laughing.

As they left the building, Katie said, "That worked better than I expected. I wish we could have gotten that other name out of him, though."

"He'll come to his senses soon," Joe said. "We should hurry out of here."

They got in the car and quickly drove away. "There's not much he can do now," Katie said.

"Don't be so sure."

It took a couple of minutes, but the euphoria O'Brian felt faded enough for him to realize what he had just done. They must have drugged him somehow. He looked out the window and saw Katie and Joe drive away. He picked up his phone and dialed a number. When it was answered, he said, "We have an emergency. A man and a woman just left here. They're driving a red Mini Cooper and heading north on 4th Street. You need to stop them and retrieve the woman's phone, or we will all go to jail."

***

"I think we should go straight to Gabe with this video," Joe said.

"I'm way ahead of you. I'm heading that way," Katie replied, her grip tightening on the steering wheel.

They passed a police car going in the other direction. In the rearview mirror, Katie saw its lights turn on as it did a U-turn. "That police car we passed turned around and is behind us now with its lights on."

Joe turned around and saw two vehicles between them and the police car. The other cars pulled over, but the police car kept coming. "Were you speeding?" Joe asked.

"No, I wasn't."

"I was afraid this might happen. I think he's a corrupt cop. O'Brian said he had a couple of cops on his payroll. I take that to mean two. One of them is dead, so this must be the one who killed Ericson's wife. Keep going and call Gabe."

"Oh, great. That's all we need: a murderer with a badge on our tail. Katie called Gabe. He answered on the first ring. "Hi, Katie. What's going on?

"We're in trouble and need your help right away."

"Of course. Where are you?"

We just left Ford's campaign headquarters on the south side. We're heading towards you on 4th Street. We have a corrupt cop behind us wanting to pull us over. We have evidence that exonerates Erickson in his wife's killing and implicates O'Brian, Ford's campaign manager. I'm sure this cop wants to take it from us. We also think he is the one who murdered Erikson's wife."

"Just a minute," Gabe said. There was a five-second pause before he said. "We're coming your way. Stay on the line. Whatever you do, don't pull over."

A traffic jam loomed ahead, forcing Katie to turn right. "I had to turn, Gabe. I'll get on Route 32."

There was a pause, and Gabe said, "Okay. We're with you."

Katie approached Route 32 just as the light turned yellow. "Hold on," she said, pressing the accelerator. The light turned red as she made a screeching left turn. In the mirror, she saw the cop delayed again by other cars. Katie kept her eyes in the mirror as the two cars behind her pulled over to let the cop go by.

"Look out!" Joe yelled. Ahead, several cars were stopped due to an accident. Katie slammed on the brakes and just missed hitting the car in the back of the line. She quickly backed up several feet, then cut through a parking lot and turned right. Unfortunately, the road dead-ended ahead. Katie promptly turned around, but she was too late. The cop parked his car at an angle, preventing her escape. She announced to Gabe where they were and urged him to hurry.

The uniformed police officer got out of his car, drew his gun, and slowly approached the driver's side of Katie's car. When he reached the window, he shouted, "Hands where I can see them!"

Katie and Joe slowly put their hands on the dashboard.

"You!" he said, pointing to Katie. "Get out of the car."

Katie opened the door and slowly got out.

The officer pointed and said, "Put your hands on the hood."

She did what he said as the officer opened her door all the way and pointed his gun at Joe. "Get out," he said.

Joe got out as the officer found Katie's purse, looked through it, and took out her phone. He placed it in his pocket. "You have no right to take that," Joe said.

He pointed his gun at Joe again and said, "Shut up. You two are in a lot of trouble. Now come over here."

Joe walked around the back of the car while the officer closed the door. He walked slowly, hoping to give Gabe time to find them. "Put your hands on the roof," the officer told Joe.

He was a tall, muscular man, relatively young, perhaps thirty. He had a tattoo of a cross on his right arm. His nametag read, "Roberts." It was a shame a young, good-looking man like that decided to throw his life away. Joe put his hands on the roof, and the officer frisked him. He then took out his handcuffs, grabbed Joe's right arm, and pulled it back. Joe resisted while he connected to the officer and found his heart. He instructed the muscle to stop beating. After a few seconds, the officer passed out and fell to the ground.

"Oh, my God!" Katie said. "Will he be okay?"

Joe took Katie's phone from the officer's pocket and handed it to her. "He'll be fine. Use your camera like before."

Katie opened the camera app and started recording while Joe restarted the man's heart. The officer slowly regained consciousness and opened his eyes. "What happened?"

"Your heart stopped," Joe said. "Apparently, someone is angry with you." He looked up to imply it was an act of God. He saw the cross and assumed the man was religious. "I think it will happen again. I can help you, but you have to tell the truth. Who sent you after us? Was it O'Brian? Are you working for him?"

"Go to hell!"

"You first," Joe said before stopping his heart again. Joe waited until he lost consciousness and then restarted his heart.

The officer opened his eyes again. There was a look of shock on his face. "What the hell? What did you do to me?"

"Hell is where you'll be going if you don't repent now."

"Who are you?"

Joe looked up at the sky and then back at the man. "I think you know. I'm here to help you, but you must help me first. Did O'Brian send you?"

He was silent for several seconds and finally said, "Yes. O'Brian sent me. He wanted me to retrieve your phone."

"Does O'Brian pay you to do his dirty work?"

The man hesitated and then nodded slowly.

"What about Erikson's wife? Did you shoot her?"

The man remained silent. "Did you shoot her?" Joe asked again. "Confession is good for the soul, if you know what I mean."

He slowly nodded. "Okay. I shot her. O'Brian paid me a lot of money, which I needed at the time."

They heard sirens as two police cars approached and stopped next to them. Katie stopped recording as Gabe got out of one of the cars. He drew his gun and pointed it at Officer Roberts as three more police officers joined him. "Are you two alright?" Gabe asked.

"Never better," Katie said. "O'Brian paid this man to kill Erikson's wife. We have the evidence here." She held up her phone.

Gabe looked at the officer and said, "Officer Roberts, you're under arrest for the murder of Patricia Erikson. Anything you say can and will be used against you in a court of law." When he finished reading his rights to him, the other officers put Roberts in the back of one of the vehicles.

"I'd like to see your evidence," Gabe said.

Katie showed him the recordings they had made. After watching them, he said, "That was great work, but you need to edit them before giving them to me. You should follow us back to the station before anything else happens to you."

As Katie was about to get in the car, Joe said. "I'll drive. You can edit those videos on the way. I assume you can do that on your phone."

"I can, but I'm not sure I want you to drive my car. I've never seen you drive before."

"I've been driving since the thirties. Just because I choose not to have a car doesn't mean I can't drive one."

Katie hesitated and said, "Fine, but you better be careful."

"You are in good hands."

Joe followed Gabe back to the police station while Katie removed the parts of the confessions that would draw attention to Joe. They arrived at the station before Katie finished, so she continued the work while sitting in Gabe's office. She then attached the videos to an email and sent them to Gabe.

When the videos arrived, Gabe watched them again and said, "Like I said, that was great work. I loved how you got confessions out of those two men. I'd like to ask how you did it, but I think I'm better off not knowing. I'll be sending someone to arrest O'Brian and Gideon Ford soon. O'Brian won't be able to wiggle his way out of this one."

"Can you wait until tomorrow before announcing the arrests?" Katie asked.

"I suppose I could do that, but why?"

"I think Mayor Ford deserves a chance to redeem himself at least somewhat."

Chapter 16

Joe and Katie met Mayor Ford at the courthouse the next morning. Katie wore a black dress that was sexy but not as revealing as some of her other outfits. She wanted to look professional. Joe wore tan slacks and a white, long-sleeved shirt. It was the only dress clothes he had packed.

Mayor Ford was able to arrange a meeting with the Judge before the trial was to resume. They had finished closing arguments the previous day, and the judge was prepared to send the jury off for deliberations.

The Judge was an older man, perhaps sixty-five, with thinning gray hair. He shook Ford's hand and said, "Good morning, Mr. Mayor."

"Good morning, your honor. I'm here with Katie and Joe Novak. They uncovered evidence proving Mr. Erickson is innocent of the crime he is accused of."

The judge looked at Katie and Joe. "Is that correct?"

"Yes, your honor," Katie said.

"Do you have this evidence with you?"

"Yes, your honor. They are recordings on my phone."

"Show them to me."

"Katie played the audio recording first and explained where it came from. She then played the two confessions."

The judge looked at Mayor Ford and said, "This will hurt your political career. I respect you for bringing this to the court's attention."

"Thank you, Your Honor," Ford said.

The judge picked up his phone and dialed a number. When it was answered, he said, "I need the prosecution and the defense in my office right away."

A few minutes later, several lawyers, as well as Daniel Erikson, were crammed into the judge's office. He said, "This young lady has some evidence you all need to see."

Katie stepped to the side of the judge's desk and held up her phone. She said, "This is Gideon Ford and Ethan O'Brian," before hitting play on the audio recorded by Bobby Parker.

The room got very quiet as everyone listened. When it was over, Erikson was visibly disturbed. He looked at Ford and said, "Wait a minute. My wife was murdered because you couldn't win an election fair and square?" He lunged toward Ford, but his lawyers held him back.

"Please," Katie said. "Mayor Ford helped us crack this case."

Erikson calmed down a bit, and Katie played the two confessions. When they finished, the judge looked at the prosecutor and said, "Mr. Dillon, would you like to say something?"

He looked down for a moment and then back up at the judge. "In light of this new evidence, Your Honor, the prosecution would like to drop the charges against Daniel Erikson."

Erikson and his lawyer hugged. Ford moved to where Erikson was standing and said, "I am so very sorry."

Erikson looked at him in disdain. "If you're looking for forgiveness, talk to a priest. You won't get it from me."

"I understand," Ford said before walking back to where Katie and Joe were standing.

"I'm sorry," Katie said.

"It wasn't unexpected. Besides, I deserve it."

"Are you ready for the next part?" Katie asked.

"I don't know," Ford said. "This will be the hardest thing I've ever done and perhaps the most liberating."

***

Ford met Katie and Joe at the news station. They went inside and up to the second floor, where the studio was located. It was halfway between the morning and the afternoon news programs. Bob Martin had a production team waiting for them. Katie and Mayor Ford both sat behind the desk. It was the first time Katie had anchored the news program.

The producer gave Katie the signal that they were live. "Good morning, Milwaukee. We are interrupting your regular programming to bring you a special report. I reported a few days ago about the murder of Robert Parker, the man who broke into Mayor Ford's home last year. It turns out that Robert Parker not only heard something he wasn't supposed to hear but also recorded it. During our investigation, we recovered that recording. It was Mayor Ford's father, Gideon Ford, conspiring with Mayor Ford's campaign manager, Ethan O'Brian, to murder Daniel Erikson's wife to get him out of the senator's race."

They waited while the recording was played for the audience. When it finished, Katie said, "There were also two Milwaukee police officers involved in the murder, one of whom was shot and killed in self-defense by his own partner."

The video cut to the two confessions that Katie recorded using her phone. When they finished playing, Katie asked, "Mayor Ford, is there anything you want to say to the people of Milwaukee?"

"Thank you, Katie. This was truly a great tragedy that I became aware of only because of your investigation. I'm not making excuses. I allowed my father to have way more power over me than I should have. I don't deserve the trust that was given to me by the great people of Milwaukee. Therefore, I am ending my campaign for the U.S. Senate. I will also be resigning as mayor, effective at noon tomorrow."

"Robert Parker was killed trying to bring this story to light," Katie said. "Do you have anything to say about that?"

"Yes. I have since learned that he broke into my home out of desperation. He was diagnosed with cancer, his wife was pregnant, and they were having trouble paying the mortgage. I also learned that my actions as mayor were directly responsible for his hours being cut at his job. Don't get me wrong. I don't condone solving problems with crime, but in Mr. Parker's case, he served his time and then tried to do the right thing to make amends. Therefore, I decided to pay Robert Parker's medical bills and help his wife, Stacy Parker, catch up on her mortgage payments. I also offered her a job at one of my jewelry stores that will pay her enough to live comfortably. In addition, Ford Jewelers will now help all our employees, like Stacy Parker, with daycare costs."

"That is very nice of you. So, what will you do now?" Katie asked.

"I'll focus all my energy on running Ford Jewelers, the only job I ever really loved. My biggest hope is that our customers can forgive me."

"I'm sure you'll see me in one of your stores sometime soon," Katie said. "For Channel 23 News, this is Katie Novak reporting."

When they finished and were off the air, Ford said, "When you're ready to make a purchase, let me know, and I'll get whatever you want for cost."

Joe was standing on the other side of the studio. Katie called to him. "Did you hear that, Honey? We can get anything we want at cost."

"Wonderful," Joe said and gave her a thumbs up.

When the report was over and Mayor Ford had left, Katie and Joe went downstairs to say goodbye to Bob Martin, Ashley, and a few other people before returning to the hotel. They both put on casual clothes and packed their suitcases. They checked out, packed the car, and headed home.

***

When they returned home, Joe brought in the luggage, and they collapsed on the sofa together. "All of this back and forth to Milwaukee is exhausting," Katie said.

"Yes, but you must feel good that we solved another murder and kept an innocent man from going to jail."

"I do feel good. Maybe we should open our own detective agency."

"Or we could focus on making the resort the best it can be."

"You're a bit of a party pooper. Wouldn't you like to be one of those old-time gumshoes?"

"That could be fun, but you are just getting started with your job, and I see great potential in you."

Katie smiled. "You're right. I do like what I do."

There was a knock at the door. Joe and Katie looked at each other. "Who could that be?" Joe asked.

"I don't know. Answer it."

Joe got up and opened the front door. Susan stood there holding a large envelope. "Susan. Come in. What are you doing here?"

Katie got up, and Susan hugged both of them. "I made a decision, Dad." She handed Joe the envelope. "I thought about giving this to you at your wedding, but I wasn't sure if the time was right. Now that you have a baby on the way, and I see how well you two work together solving crimes, I feel so proud of all the progress you've made lately."

"What are you getting at, Susan?"

"Open the envelope."

Joe opened the envelope and pulled out several pieces of paper. "It's the deed to the resort and all my investments. You put them back in my name. Why?"

"After Mom died, you were a mess for years. You faked your death, changed your name again, and hid out in that cabin of yours most of the time. When you left everything to me, it felt like you were giving up. I always thought you needed time, and I would return everything to you when you were ready. Of course, I didn't expect it to take twenty years, but I think you're ready now. Since you met Katie, you have returned to being the happy, responsible man I once knew." She looked at Katie and smiled.

"I don't know what to say," Joe said. "I guess I have changed since meeting Katie. I feel like I have a purpose again."

Katie and Joe hugged. "He's still like a child sometimes," Katie said, "but I can handle him."

"I know you can, Katie. You are exactly what he needs."

"Would you like to stay for a while?" Katie asked.

"Oh, no. I know you two must be tired. I'll let you relax. I'll be working tomorrow. We can talk more then."

When Susan left, Katie said, "That was nice of her. Were you really that much of a mess? Besides being a hermit, I thought you were relatively normal when we met."

"I was never a hermit. I just liked solitude."

"Like a hermit."

"The answer to your question is yes. I was messed up. At first, I didn't know how to be alone. I was never alone my entire life until then. After a while, I didn't know how to be with other people. I stopped working at the resort for several years, but then gradually started working again part-time. I was lucky Susan was there to step into the manager role, and then Michael when she retired. Marie and I did that together, but she was always better at the boring paperwork stuff."

"I can't imagine what you went through."

"Fortunately, that's all in the past. Can we talk about something else?"

"We can talk about that big tax burden you will have now."

"Please, anything but that."

"Okay. How about we feel the baby again?"

"Now you're talking my language," Joe said. They held hands as Joe connected with Katie. They both concentrated on the tiny life growing inside her.

"Can you tell if she's a boy or a girl yet?" Katie asked.

Joe concentrated hard for several seconds and finally said, "Sorry. I can't tell yet."

Katie concentrated hard, too, and, after a long pause, said, "He's a boy. Our baby is a boy."

"He is? How do you know?"

"Because I know you. I know what you feel like, and this baby feels like you."

"I'm impressed," Joe said. "It looks like we solved another mystery today."

I truly appreciate you taking the time to read Last Chance. I hope you enjoyed following Katie and Joe on their latest mystery.

I would be incredibly grateful if you left a review on Amazon, Goodreads, or wherever you purchased this book. Your thoughts help other readers discover the series and mean a lot to me as an author. Whether it's a few words or a detailed review, your feedback makes a difference.

Thank you again for your support. I couldn't do this without readers like you.

Charles Huss

Books In This Series

Last Healer Mysteries

Joe, a reclusive, ageless centenarian, meets Katie, an ambitious news personality with dreams of being an investigative reporter. Together, they solve crimes and explore the full potential of Joe's healing abilities while navigating the complexities of their intimate relationship.

Book One - The Last Healer

On the eve of her thirtieth birthday, Katie, a television news reporter, unhappy with her career and her love life, decides to spend the weekend alone at a Wisconsin ski resort.

Joe is a man content to live a private life in his cabin in the woods. Since the death of his wife, he has avoided intimate relationships and prefers to keep a low profile to prevent people from learning of his unusual abilities.

On the way to the ski resort, Katie makes a wrong turn during a snowstorm and hits Joe with her car. Lost and with no cell signal, Katie tries to keep Joe alive until she can get help. During Joe's recovery, Katie learns his secret and soon helps to investigate his family's mysterious past while Joe helps Katie investigate a double murder. Love blossoms while they slowly unravel both mysteries, but danger lies ahead. Can Joe discover the full extent of his abilities before it is too late?

Book Two - Last Rites

In this gripping sequel to "The Last Healer," Katie and Joe, fresh from their honeymoon, must race to Milwaukee to save the life of Katie's dear friend Ashley after she and her mother fall victim to a ruthless attack. With Ashley on the brink of death while a priest delivers Last Rites, her only chance for survival is Joe's remarkable healing powers.

What starts as a rescue mission turns into a murder investigation as they investigate the killing of Ashley's mother. While searching for the shooter, their investigation leads them to a chilling conspiracy centered on the city's homeless population. As they uncover more of the truth, they become targets as someone is determined to silence them. Will Katie and Joe find who is behind a series of murders, or will they become the next victims?

Book 3 – Last Chance

In Book Three of the Last Healer Mysteries, Katie and Joe, after deciding to quit investigating murders, are thrust back into it when a man is murdered at Joe's resort.

The victim is no ordinary man. He is a suspected jewel thief, believed to have hidden stolen jewels at the resort. While they struggle to handle all the treasure seekers, Katie and Joe debate how involved they should be in the murder investigation. They don't know the killer lurks in the background, taking orders from some of the most powerful people in Wisconsin while he waits for Katie and Joe to find what he is looking for.

Book 4 – Last Flight

In Book Four of the Last Healer Mysteries series, Katie and Joe witness the deadly crash of a prototype aircraft and save the life of one of its occupants. After Joe discovers evidence of sabotage, Katie insists she can investigate the crime despite being almost nine months pregnant.

Someone planted an explosive device in the aircraft, killing the company's founder and jeopardizing the struggling startup's future. Was the attack meant to destroy the company, or was it something more personal? As Katie and Joe hit one dead end after another, they discover the killer isn't finished. With time running out, they race to save the next victim, but with people dying, a murderer on the loose, and Katie in labor, what's a Healer to do?

Book 5 – Last Hope (Coming Soon)

In book five of the Last Healer Mysteries series, Katie and Joe are celebrating their son's first birthday when they learn the husband of Katie's childhood best friend has been arrested for murdering the small town's only police detective. They return to Katie's hometown, determined to find the real killer.

As they dig deeper, they uncover chilling ties between the detective's death and the recent killing of the mayor's daughter. It soon becomes clear someone will do anything to keep the truth buried.

Other Books By Charles Huss

Truth Be Told

Peter Beckett awoke 25 years ago with no memory of his past. Since then, he's been haunted by a gift he never asked for and doesn't want. People can't lie to him. To Peter, it feels like a curse that has left him isolated and feared by all who get to know him. Only his priest accepts him for who he is.

The FBI has been watching him, and they need his unique talent to track a deadly drug cartel that has infiltrated Milwaukee, fueling a dangerous spike of fentanyl overdoses. Rookie agent Hannah Meyers is assigned to recruit Peter, who is reluctant to help, but is intrigued by Hannah after she lies to him.

As the investigation deepens, details of Peter's former life emerge. With secrets unraveling and lives on the line, Peter must decide whether to return to the glorious life he once knew or give it all up for love.

Saving Apollo

Apollo is no ordinary dog. Along with his sister, Athena, he was genetically modified to be smarter than a chimpanzee. When the lead geneticist quits over a dispute about the fate of the dogs, chaos erupts, and Apollo escapes, ending up on a small island off the Florida coast. There, he befriends twelve-year-old Ethan, who has just moved to the island with his dad, Ryan.

As they uncover Apollo's extraordinary ability to understand them, they also learn about the perilous fate that awaits him if he returns. With the help of their neighbor, Brooke, a local veterinarian, they devise a plan to save Apollo and Athena. Standing in their way is Jack Strauss, a former Marine and head of security at the lab that created Apollo and Athena.

"Saving Apollo" is a heartwarming, family-friendly story of friendship, love, and compassion.

Falling Star

A meteorite crashes into the serene wilderness of a national park. In its aftermath, both people and animals succumb to aggressive behavior followed by death. Two rookies, FBI agent Beth Hartley and Park Ranger Mike Bauer, are put together to investigate the strange events.

Beth is tough as they come on the outside but vulnerable on the inside. After her last breakup, she has given up on men to focus on her career. Mike, a former military police officer, has developed trust issues and prefers his new career where he has no partner that he needs to rely on.

As their investigation brings them closer to the truth, they find themselves getting closer to each other. In a dangerous forest where every animal is a potential threat, and even the air could be toxic, their best chance for survival is a partner they can trust.

Identity Crisis

After Alex Neumann agrees to participate in his father's groundbreaking memory recording experiment, he awakens years later to find he is not the man he used to be. He soon becomes a pawn in a deadly scheme involving a ruthless businessman, an Army general, and the President of The United States.

As Alex peels away layers of deception, his true identity slowly emerges, along with skills foreign to his old self. He will need all those skills and the help of friends he meets along the way to survive and turn the tables on his adversaries.

Bad Cat Chris: The Baddest Cat You'll Ever Love

When Chuck volunteered to help a local cat shelter clean cages one morning, the last thing he expected was a kitten climbing up his back to perch on his shoulders, but that was the beginning of a relationship that would test the limits of human endurance and compassion.

This is the story of Chris, a cat like no other who would turn the lives of Chuck and Rose upside-down while eventually showing them that bad can be good and love can come from the most unlikely places.

This book is based on Chris's blog at BadCatChris.com and is a collection of sometimes serious but mostly humorous stories about the ups and downs of living with a bad cat.

About The Author

Charles Huss was born and raised in the suburbs of Chicago but has lived most of his adult life in the Tampa Bay, Florida, area. He is a graduate of St. Petersburg College and is the author of several books. He currently lives with his wife, Rose, and their two cats.

Don't miss out!

Visit the website below and you can sign up to receive emails whenever Charles Huss publishes a new book. There's no charge and no obligation.

https://books2read.com/r/B-A-LHRY-TGHQD

BOOKS 2 READ

Connecting independent readers to independent writers.

Did you love *Last Chance*? Then you should read *Last Flight*[1] by Charles Huss!

[2]

In book four of the Last Healer Mysteries series, Katie and Joe witness the deadly crash of a prototype aircraft and save the life of one of its occupants. After Joe discovers evidence of sabotage, Katie insists she is capable of investigating the crime despite being almost nine months pregnant.

Someone planted an explosive device in the aircraft, killing the company's founder and jeopardizing the struggling startup's future. Was the attack meant to destroy the company, or was it something more personal? As Katie and Joe hit one dead end after another, they learn the killer isn't finished.

With time running out, they race to save the next victim, but with people dying, a murderer on the loose, and Katie in labor, what's a Healer to do?

Read more at charleshuss.com.

---

1. https://books2read.com/u/mqoRJ8

2. https://books2read.com/u/mqoRJ8

www.ingramcontent.com/pod-product-compliance
Lightning Source LLC
Chambersburg PA
CBHW050901180626
46814CB00007B/2831